MW00444732

I WILL CRASH

by the same author

LITTLE SCRATCH

REBECCA WATSON

I WILL CRASH

faber

First published in 2024
by Faber & Faber Limited
The Bindery, 51 Hatton Garden
London EC1N 8HN

Typeset by Faber & Faber Limited
Printed and bound by CPI Group (UK) Ltd, Croydon, CR0 4YY

A CIP record for this book
is available from the British Library

*All characters, names, places and events in this book are fictitious
and any resemblance to persons living or dead, places or events
is entirely coincidental.*

ISBN 978–0–571–35674–4

Printed and bound in the UK on FSC® certified paper in line with our continuing
commitment to ethical business practices, sustainability and the environment.
For further information see faber.co.uk/environmental-policy

2 4 6 8 10 9 7 5 3 1

For James

I WILL CRASH

I opened the door, and there he was   my brother
                                         face carefully neutral.

                                   Alright, he said.

He was older, definitely
of course he was   nobody escapes time
but he looked it   not in lines or wear

something about him was fuller
more real than my imagination would allow.

It had been six years
enough had passed that I could notice
otherwise, it would have been only him
                          but instead,
                                         there was difference

everything a little changed

        except that stubborn patch of skin above his left temple
        just as I remembered, puckered yellow.

It was a peace offering, I knew that
as I tried to swallow the affront of him being there
while he waited for my response

you don't appear on someone's doorstep uninvited,
                                         saying Alright

unless you want to make amends
            even if it was a grunt of a word, Alright
            leaving me, really, to be the first to speak.

I thought you were the postman
that's what I said   at first   my mouth ahead of me.

He kept standing there   uninvited
                                           wrinkled forehead
I didn't invite him in, but I could have
there are always alternatives.

Hey, I could have said,
Come in.
Here's my brother, I could have said
muttering it to myself
as I walked back up the stairs   him following,
                                       just behind.

Here's my brother, under my breath
introducing him to the furniture,
making it real, casual, ordinary.

                        Here I am,
                        he would say.
Here I am.

We would have warmed up. Settling on something safe.
One quick memory.
I saw Dad last week, Dad and the rodent.

Jesus christ. A laugh (from him).
Rich, deep chuckle.
How is that bloody dog still alive?

A simple start, it had to be. Edging back towards each other.

This was not the first attempt
each one botched in its own way
                          this one, in the closing of the door.

No,   I said
it was nearly all I could manage
No,   sorry,   no,   I said.

Come on, he called at me in an almost yelp,
standing there for something unknown   (now lost)
his expression broke, voice loud and high
(too late the decision was already made)

                                        Don't just—

I didn't hear the rest.

No,   sorry,   no,   I said
and closed the door.

Yes, there were alternatives.
We could have started gently. Nerves, anticipation.
A gesture. Easy. You're here, come in.

Could have, should have, didn't.
Closed the door.

I closed it, and I kept my hand on the wood.
Flat against, waiting.

His shadow on the other side,
a dark smudge
blocking door crack

no light let in

then receding

I didn't just shut the door   I smiled
master of the situation.

There were alternatives.

There always are.

But the real pieces

him at the door

saying no

then gone

those are set bones

I can do nothing with them other than admit that they are there.

Wednesday

Dad calls, and I know.
I know, I know, fuck, I know.
As though I am being reminded of a memory, it rises
familiar, settling over me as if it has before.

Yes, right, of course, he's dead.

Did you hear me?

Yes, I did. But I have heard it before.

Haven't I? I know. He's dead, I know.

Yes, Dad, are you okay? I say.

My words sound rehearsed.

Car crash, Dad says.
His voice is tentative, caught in the conflict of having to
speak it. Somehow turning it intimate, not this, not really,
not the fact. Not the brutality, the harshness. No, soft.

Car crash . . .
I am in the car with him. With my brother.

Younger. How have I forgotten?

It was why I have always refused to get in a car with him since.

But a story I never told   (perhaps how it has stayed down)
too cruel in paraphrase   he threatened to kill us both.
A good beginning, maybe, but hardly the truth

too uncomplicated.

It wasn't anger, not at first, it was only that he was accustomed
to getting what he wanted.

Going into town for different nights,
Dad had said,   Why don't you take your sister
                                        if you're going the same way?
I didn't look up, waiting for the No
so I heard the grin before I saw it.
                                        Sure, of course,
                                        come along for a ride.

When we were in the car   seat belts!
                            doors locked, acceleration
the grin began to make sense
                            What's Alice's phone number?
                            Put it in my phone.

Alice was my best friend,
the girl to be measured against
at school, beauty is fixed,
numbers are attached,
Alice was the top measurement.

No, I said   (my fault
                                    for what comes next
                                    I did say no)
Ask her yourself, I said.

He could've, couldn't he?   He could have asked her.

But he had decided how it was going to work.
That was the point. He had decided.

Give me her number.

He was not asking a question, he was demanding.
But he was driving!   me on the passenger side,
                      arms crossed
                      seat belt crossed
I was safe.

No, I repeated, it's her number to give.
And she's two years below you,

I paused over the ending, then delivered
                              you creep.

He rested on the word. Creep, he said. Feeling it in his mouth.
Eyes on the road. Lights hitting tarmac.
Not able to see beyond. Creep.

I was pushing back but I didn't want to hurt him.
Always hard to balance. I'm not trying to be a dick, I said.
Quietly, reluctant to give him the words.
                    I just think it's fairer if you ask her.

The creep disagrees, he said.

Give me her number
            or

                         hovering
                         not yet, not yet
                         but something approaching
I'll crash the car.

He didn't shout, which was how I knew he meant it

otherwise, he would have presented his words differently,
the threat needing performance to make up for no intent.

It was serious, but I had begun my no, and I had to try
I had to keep at my no, no, no
if I always stopped, sure it wouldn't work, it never would.

No, I repeated. It's her number to give.

He sighed then, though sighed sounds too calm
it was an angry shunt of breath
exhaled with finality, acting like a switch:
it was me, making him do this,   I made him do this,

                    as he wrenched the steering wheel to the side
        veering

First, an attempt to scare.

He wasn't ready, I could see that as I put my hand on the
side of the wheel, trying to ground us both.
Not yet. There was still time to change his course.

Stop it, I shouted. Are you fucking crazy?

Did you   he said through a set mouth   or didn't you
hear   eyes ahead, not looking   me?

Give me her number or I'll crash the car.

Accelerating then. Jerking across
                            the painted dashes on the road.
No one coming, only emphasising our vulnerability.

He had got this from Mum, I knew. Pulling the memory out
of shape. Mum had joked when we were tiny: long empty road,
shouting (softly)
OH GOD, I'VE LOST CONTROL!
Teasing as she swerved gently, until one time.
My brother began to fill, reddening, with unclear fury,
mystifying yet uncontainable, screaming to release.
No words, just screams.

Still roaring as Mum stopped on the side of the road and
picked him out of the car. I watched her march into the field.
Nagging shoulder, his legs in the air.
Alone in the car, I could hear a window-muted cry,
Mum's face determined as she spun around and around
                                          and around.

He was stealing her trick and I was tempted to steal his
response: screaming, screaming, screaming.

But as he accelerated, facing forward
as I shouted at him that he was being   Fucking insane!
and as he kept on, grinning as if that was justification

I knew there was no joke

it was a test   a bet he had with himself
if he shouldn't   then he had to

Give me her number.   Give me her number.
Give me her number.   Give me her number.

All I had   he knew   was Alice's number.
Nothing else was relevant, there was no way out
I knew it   shouting FINE
sharp and loud to force it out of my mouth.

The quicker I agreed the quicker he might stop, and he did. Just
as Mum had done when he had screamed his endless scream.

                    Car crash.

As Dad speaks, I sit down.
Firm wood of the chair under me
                              I don't choose to   but suddenly
hand against the counter to keep me upright   I have to

tremor of my legs surprising me   scaring me

Dad's voice is reedy, speaking into what I know.

Of course he would die driving,
he cared for nothing, not even himself
if he did, he would have been kinder, if only for his own sake
if he cared then he wouldn't throw himself at people with
unrestricted anger   with no concern for self-preservation
he wouldn't accelerate without thinking of brakes

I knew   I'm sure I already knew.

Hearing doesn't click anything into place, I don't start crying,
say No Dad, no, it had been raining, heavy, clouds low, and
of course he had been driving too fast, of course he had been
driving down the motorway like it was a fucking game, no
limits, never any limits, of course he was alone, he never kept
friends, couldn't,   why would death be any different

why would he die with anyone other than himself?

Twisted   I don't remember how I say goodbye
I sound more like him than me
                          off the phone, clicked shut in my hand

                fuck   fuck   fuck

head against the table

                fuck   fuck   fuck

It's a death   you know this

death is a death is a death is a death

                    you know this

Invisible lines across my scalp, building a lattice
like someone has poured water
slowly, slyly over my head, striking the crown

spreading like liquid, maybe, but the feeling   tightening
like someone has grabbed at the end of my hair hard
no limits   straining to stay attached

eyelids heavy against me
colours of the kitchen   white of cabinet,
                                      red of chopping board
light hitting the table   buffing to a blinding shine

even a framed poster   usually mute in sepia
                                      usually calm on the wall
spits at me   black of its inscription severe

                                      I can't deal with any of it
none of me can

music from the speaker an insistent wasp

                                      suspended knowledge

knowing already I will never be able to listen to this song again
even though her voice has always been soothing,
would never have the capacity to sound how she does now
                                    grating, harsh, horrible

all exaggerated by, what, as if I am anticipating something but
no

that behind   that behind   he's dead

everything new, unknown, as if under spotlight
                                magnifying glass
all too much
yet all of it already behind me   already, I am ahead

what I know is simple   is fact   is in the past
                                    happened

I hadn't thought to ask   had Dad seen him?
he must have gone to identify
Dad keeping to thin information   not wanting me to imagine

How do I even?

I am sitting at the kitchen table, onions cut,
beginning to peel garlic. October.
It is October. He was here a few weeks ago. On the threshold.

His death is not something only to feel, but to tell.

John is out but he'll be back. Before midnight, likely.
Many beers down, likely.

How do I even   tell this?

Not yet   how to even explain   he'll be drunk

he'll be   none of it him, really   me   I'll be
                                                askew

stuttering, jittered   can't

If John was here, he would know. Tone is enough.
Phone calls announcing someone has died have their own
theatre: voice prepared, unable to stall.

You only have to be there to know.

'Hello—' cut off

                'Fuck'

                                'Oh god'

        'What happened?'

It's the abruptness you sense   the efficiency of death

the person on the other end of the phone already tired
while preparing for the next call   sitting there
                                     with a list of names
ready to say: I'm so sorry, he's dead
before preparing to tell the next   I'm so sorry, he's dead.

If John was here   I wouldn't need to tell him

he would be ready, he could help me decode.

                                            'It's my brother'

That would be enough.

Instead: how?

Better to let him come home when he's ready

in bed, I'll whisper it to him   we'll fall asleep
explain more in the morning

that way, I'll get to tell it in halves

when John gets home   drunk, tired, him
slurring as he toasts bread from the freezer
breaking apart rigid white slices

I can't.

He is child-drunk: doting, simple, easy to win grins.
He puts his hands out to me and repeats my name,

Rosa,

                    Rosa,

                                        Rosa.

I want this   I don't want to cut through it,
I want these last moments of living past.

How was work? he asks.
A question I can answer.
Oh you know: braying kids, the smell of potato and bleach.
Margo read three pages of a book to me without a single mess-up,
which in school terms
is what we call a miracle.   Catches my throat, that
                                        I had been touched earlier
                                        amazed, proud

                                        but this   foreign
let the tears in my eyes be Margo,   that
                                                          is what it is

You're so good, he says, kissing my cheek
                          leaving a hint of pub.
I am, I say, *but I'm knackered.*
Teaching done for the week now, he says,
tomorrow we'll be right here.

He pulls me onto his lap,
strokes my hair,
eats toast like a baby bird.

Content, quiet.

For a moment, my timelines are out of sync.
Why would I correct that?

I don't consider what it means for tomorrow
all I know is once more my brother is not dead
I don't even have a brother
just us.

I'm going to get into bed,   I say
he strokes my stomach,   then releases me
                                      gently pushing me up.

See you in there, he says absent-mindedly,

as he slots another slice in the toaster
chin against his chest in concentration
comical,
the difference between sober and drunk
fractional shift turning ordinary absurd.

Everything is as it was   it's all I need to think.
Everything is as it was   but my legs have other plans.
Everything instead theoretical
guiding myself to the bathroom to brush my teeth
none of it real dreamlike   not even nightmarish yet
just
moving through a delay
time,
me,
all waiting to catch up.

Watch this.

That's what he had said, my brother
mischief close behind.
Watch this,

a redundant command
I was guaranteed to follow, guaranteed to watch
then, it was automatic, my comrade in the grand war of living
(when the war was not between us but so clearly beyond, it was
us against everything purely for the glee of being a united front)
Mum (he had said louder) fuck off!

It was delivered sweetly, his face alight
trouble should have set in
but it was hard when he was beaming
he had said it as if he were saying, I love you
Mum creased, unable to resist
                Fuck off, I said, his backing singer
                fuck off, fuck off, fuck off.
                Now Rosa, she said, collecting herself.
Back to being Mum
                One fuck off token a year I think, and look,
                there's mine gone. Both of your tokens too.

In bed, just us, the silence begins to oppress
forming a barrier against sleep
my body is too insistent on wriggling
I lie on my back,   ankle flexing
if I can't sleep, I can at least let John
no, ankle stay, body stay, don't roll

                but I want to move,
                my ankle says,
                in its twitching

        this is not how I want to spend my night,
        front slope of foot says,
        brushing against the duvet
        is it fair to make me spend my night like this?

John's face is towards me, crumpled, cheek pushed against the pillow, before he rolls too, turning away from me.

Awake? Asleep? Hard to tell, his breathing still even but faint, not breathy, not deep, maybe awake, maybe.

Lying on my side, the itches return. Of course they do, stupid ankle, stupid arm, stupid stiffening shoulder blades. I am never going to find the right position. It is not that I am not thinking of myself, but if each movement is pointless, if I am never going to find the right position, then yes, I should stay still, ignoring each part of my body until the urges dim, and before then, at least someone will sleep, even if it isn't me not me, certainly　　　　no sent to　　　　　　school gates

Alice　　　　　　　　　didn't know her name then
　　　　　　　　　　　　didn't have her number either.

Just another girl wearing a sequinned clip to keep her hair behind her ear, hers on the left, mine on the right, like we were mirrored images

I don't remember how I replied when she nudged my arm
and said,　　　　　　　It's Wed-nes-day.
I might have laughed or ducked my head or said
Wensday! You pronounce it Wens-day!

even though I would have known　　　　　quick
seen how her tongue poked just a little under her teeth

pure silliness, Alice, I knew already
before she had even said her name
which she did, Alice, she said after that, didn't she

       I'm Alice.

       If you give me your clip

       I'll have a pair.

Hi Alice, I said.
If I give you my clip, I'll have none.

I remember how she thought on that, teasing at her bottom lip.

       Let's swap, she said, and we did

       her sliding the clip against my scalp

hair pulled too taut   stretching from the roots

           the strain of it.

You cannot count time in the dark.
It passes, impossibly
there are no markers of how long it's been
nothing to judge whether it's crawling, speeding,
flaking off minute by minute

lying there tense itching
my body tells me I am resisting
      listen
listen!   fucking listen!

My body contains what I will not think about
but I don't listen.

Thursday

Wake up to John stroking my arm
edge of nail scuffing skin

it's there, waiting for me

                                        Your brother is dead
jesus
at least give me one second's delay

I have to tell him
there's no reason left

Tell him   My brother is dead

they're only words   you have them ready
except
difficult to speak once the gap has begun
not last night   why this morning?

John pulls me in
chin locked onto my shoulder
Mmmmm, he says
the sound of warmth

I say nothing   teeth tight in my lip
(the sound of a secret)

I can't start with anything other than the truth
the specific truth   My brother is dead
not that today is Thursday

or that finally   I reached a blank sleep, out like a corpse
or how   if I narrow my eyes
                    while looking at the painting on the wall
                    the landscape turns to dreamscape
                    outline of a tree like an overgrown blowfish
not that either, no
                    I've told him before, anyway.
                    Can you see that fish? I've asked.
                    Squint your eyes and tell me.

No reason why I'd tell him a second time,
not when more pressing things
are yet to be said

Wasting time
circling around, preparing the words only to start again

                                        My brother is dead
nothing else first

he touches his nose to my cheek
(reacting to my silence   or else, my body   tense as steel)

Mmmm?   a question
I make my mouth move
                         how have I kept it shut?

Cutting through, chopping words out quick.

He's dead,   I say   nonsense into my pillow

What did you say?

My brother,   I say   louder   trying now
Dad called and told me, that he died.

Unbelievable to think of the delay,
now it's been said

I regret the mess, bringing it to life in a scrambled mouthful

Sweetheart fuck what happened   startled, alert   then
when did you find out?   bringing his voice back to soft

face wet hot not mine
body always telling on me

walked into school the morning after my grandma died
feeling altered
while exactly the same
only when Alice turned to me in class and said Okay what is it?
could I connect myself at the desk with me from the night
before crying in bed
                    My grandma died, I said
the words reacting in my mouth, forming and upset forming
with them, face contracting, unsure how I could contain.

33

Alice took my hand and pulled me up past the desks,
past Mrs Clark   (Miss, we need the toilet, she said,
                                   not waiting for a response)
while my teeth gripped the inside of my cheeks,
clamping my face together.

               The shallow thud of toilet lid, Alice beckoning
               I sat on her lap   teenager playing child
               crying as she brushed my hair with her fingers
               shushing me, knowing how to soothe.

John hugs me when I cry too much to answer
only crying more when I start to think about my brother clearly
him dead, no longer here
no longer   I find myself thinking   trying to stop.

I am safe now.

Doubtful how much I needed to be freed.
Unsure whether I had ever been unsafe.

John hugs me, bringing me into him
cocooned

my brother had hurt me   I have to remember

I cannot forget

               I can be sad

but I cannot allow myself to be destroyed
he didn't deserve that

I explain in half-statements
last night, Dad called, car crash, gone
punctuating each fact
with bullet-point sobs

my body reacts against what I say

I can't believe it yet
the shock of it
It's so much to take in, Rosa, it won't sink in, not yet.
As he rubs my hair, I feel him easing me
he smells sour, doubly slept, last night's beer close.

I sit up   back against the headboard
he shifts with me
my shoulder fitting against his chest
peaceful, his arm enclosing me
unreal   all of it
how was that real   how was I unable to say something
as simple as   my brother is dead
how is it   that he is
fake,   numb words.

Dad didn't go into details but they called him, he must have had
to go and identify   horrible to think about it I don't even know
who found him   someone was the first to find out

to see his car, to get up close, to think for a moment maybe
whoever was in there might be okay, that there was some chance

all of that just happened without me knowing, all of it condensed
into a phone call with Dad, all of it condensed into

face hot again   impossible, surely

It's horrible, Ro, horrible, and a horrible shock too, I'm so sorry
it's natural to be stunned.

I nod   it helps
stunned   that is what I am, isn't it?

I focus on him   feel his arm   this is real

here we are.

God I'm so tired.
Returning my back to flat against the mattress.
Mmm, I say, head heavy, cradled in the pillow
                              letting my eyes shut down
You could try and go back to sleep, sweetheart?
Mmm, I say,   yes, I think   I will

                              pulse in my left eyelid
                              duvet against my cheek

                    drifting

slipping back

at first there is just inky thickness like black treacle

rolling over and over until it splits
                        movement disturbing something, opening,
making a sliver of red that widens becoming shapes water
trickling through towards me, faster, sweeping me up unable to
shift my legs, my arms sewn to my sides, paralysed by the rush

I'll drown eventually
but I have to wait
nothing is immediate.

Cold hard buzz   heaving awake

someone at the door
bed empty except for me
no evidence of John
I lurch out, heartbeat catching up, put on dressing gown,
get moving, all with the abruptness that
                                my brother is dead

alongside that, fear
someone at the door
                fear
it wouldn't make sense   it couldn't
                                my brother is dead

yet   fuck
moving down the stairs   (surely not?)

surely not   (breathing)
surely not?
my heart like a mouse trying to escape.

I make my way down the stairs   heart
taking each one slowly, carefully, factually   insisting
foot, step, next
Dead people remain dead   just a reminder
in case you have forgotten   a recap
dead people remain dead
just because your brother once turned up uninvited
doesn't mean he will again
an important lesson   a lesson for all, really
                                       one of expectation

not your brother,   step
            not your brother,   step
                        not your brother,   step.

The gesture of opening the door is expansive
as I twist the latch, I see:
                    my brother
                    SURPRISE, I survived

                    my brother
                    hands out, ready to capture my throat

                    my brother, a zombie,
                    skin clammy as he moves close

as I twist the latch, I see:

my mum,

I'm sorry sweetheart, I'm sorry,

I blame myself

I see   everyone, everything

(except)

what I do not see is what I meet

Hello!

We're passing by to share an

not him, not her,   *important message. If you take*

not anything   *a look at what it says here—*

Jehovah's fucking Witnesses

Sorry,

I wipe my nose with the rough of my hand

I wouldn't have answered the door

only, I thought you might be my dead brother.

They look at each other, then back to me

One says,   *Okay here's a leaflet.*

Other says, *Sorry to bother you.*

One says,   *Have you read Matthew—*

I say,   *Yes, well, no, I haven't*

but I need to go now,

I've   I pause

looking down at my dressing gown

got a conference call.

Other says, *A conference call?*

Yes, I say, emboldened   professional
suddenly corporate   speaking briskly
you know how it is.

I close the door
                    oh god not him
of course not him
how could it possibly be him
death is a death   not a man at the door ready to surprise
                          not a man at the door ready to say
                          Well here I am! Special delivery:
                          one dead brother still alive.

Who was that?   John, there

Where have you been?
unintended desperation
I hear it too late
see it in how rapidly he is near

his arms a foil blanket tucked around me

It's okay, he says.
I'm fine,   I say,
but my head is grinding   too much within,
                                     too much to restrain

I need to sit down now   sinking down
                                    top of stairs

Just breathe for a moment.

I want to scoff   I know to fucking breathe
I want to say   fuck off, fuck off
push away for no reason
but I'm not so sure I do   know to breathe

not really, I need prompting

                                        swallowing, fuck off, fuck off
                                        like some broken instinct

breathing for a moment, just like he suggested
head in hands, a cliché of grief

he's right,
breathe

letting myself steady,
breathe   Alice,

                              so long ago now
                              distant, closer to when
                              falling might be expected

                              that car racing past
                              the fright making her topple

she was just ahead
and I stopped pedalling, transfixed

before closing the distance

her knees bleeding, her eyes out of focus, remember,
how cast in ice I was, too solid to think,
saying, Are you okay, sure, but no intuition
it was only when someone passed and said,
Would you like me to call someone, here's some water,
she's bleeding she should get cleaned up,
only then, yes, right, this is what I should do

later Alice's mum called
that soft rasp of her voice against my ear
she had said delicately yet certainly
Thank you thank you thank you
for what, I didn't ask

        if no one had passed we would still be there
        my hand on Alice's shoulder
        are you okay are you okay are you okay?

Then I thought,   bad friend
now I think,   you would be an awful mother.

        You'd drag them down.
        You and baby
        both fucked up.

Back to bed.
John sits on my side,
scrutinising me.

Head rush, I say.
Got out of bed fast
ran to get the door.

I don't say
I ran
because
I was convinced
it was my brother.

You stay here,
I'm making us coffee and toast.
I retreat under the duvet
Thank you.

Day already derailed. We had imagined it earlier in the week.
He would be hungover, we would work from home.
Tomorrow he was leaving for the conference.
Today he'd practise his keynote,
while I worked on ideas for my column

           the precious part of my week beginning
           away from the classroom

usually I'd feel that thrill   back to me   that was the feeling
back to him too,   sitting next to each other
letting my hand rest on the nape of his neck,
noticing the softness beneath his hair

                                    My brother is dead
always hard to plan for interruptions

I imagine him across the room
switching expressions, like he is dancing with me
if I scowl   him grinning

he makes his way past my sentences
in the forefront
almost making an entrance

   THAT BOY NEVER FAILS TO MAKE
   AN ENTRANCE
   Dad always provoked
   Dad. He's a teenager. Remember.
   He's got things on his mind. How to turn a key quietly
   in a lock when he's got spots to pop. In he would come.
   Then Dad, Oh! I didn't know you were back!
   (Dad, come on.)

   Never learning quiet
     tumbling around
I make him sound like a fat man with a drum
                    like a puffed-up grape
that sending me   (rebounding)
seeing him   he always used to   grape
        chucked up in the air   mouth open
ready to catch

I don't picture him, not exactly
but there's something
                                  lingering
like he's listening in

how have I spent so much of my time
not thinking of him

yet I can't imagine the possibility
                         that he could just be   not here.

I'm going to lie right by you, John says
and we are going to drink this coffee
and eat this toast
and feel just a little better.

This sounds sensible, I say
you are sensible, I say, putting my weight behind 'you'.

Do you think I'm weird
for not telling you last night?

It's a relief to ask, even if the answer is yes,
yes, you're fucking mental
it's still a relief.

It's my fault, he says
I should have asked how you were.

No, I say,
Yes, he says, and we overlap, softly but insistently,
No, Yes, No, Yes, No, until he breaks off an edge of toast
and butts it (kindly) against my mouth.
Yes, he says, *now eat*.

I have slipped him fragments

I have said before: my brother hurt me, bullied me, made
growing up destructive, difficult, something to escape from,
hard to know what sticks

the first time John learnt about my brother
I was unprepared.

Usually I would know what to say, not the first time I've had
to answer, no, people ask about siblings more than someone
unbothered would expect
an easy go-to at work, meeting someone new, around
Christmas, birthdays, oh yes,
yet that time, I hadn't anticipated
I had imagined that I didn't need to bring him in yet,
that somehow I had a guaranteed delay.
It didn't make any sense   what could be buying me time?
but that is what I thought   hoped, at least

when I was with him, with John, there was a distance
I didn't need to be anything other than me   the me now

46

                                                            right from the start
moved away from my beginnings, from all of it.

So yes, the first time John learnt about my brother I was
unprepared. The two of them were incongruous.

We had met at the gated slope of Finsbury Park
me, with a picnic rug and strawberries
John, with four cans of Kronenbourg
and an air of timid apology

the right of my mouth had smiled itself into a smirk
I stood in front of him by the entrance and he said,
Hey you.
We kept standing
looking at each other   in the pause before
something surreal, time-slowing about the sight of each other

              Do I still look alright now you're sober?
              I voiced concern like a tease.
              Gorgeous, he said, and bent down to kiss me.

Only quick.
Enough to be reminded of the warmth of his mouth.

It was after he had pulled two beers from their plastic rings
passing mine, opening his
after the soundless cheers
that we began to talk about growing up: how we had both

come from small towns, neither of us rushing back to visit,
none of that nostalgia others overflow with
he had mentioned his dad
(difficult, unpleasant, embarrassing to be honest)
it was after that, just as I was thinking of my brother
that he asked
So you're an only child too?

In not mentioning, I had meant to stall
but instead, I had drawn attention,

and I was unprepared.

Yes, I said, No, I said.
Make your mind up, he joked.
Then raised his eyebrows in anticipation of an answer.

One brother. Couple of years older. Politely estranged.
Ah. Right. That sounds like something.

Sure is. He's something. Yes. Something.
It's been stop-and-start, but in the past year, well,
I've drawn a line.

I had been lying down, him sitting up
his head tilted towards me
but he stretched onto his belly at that
and said,
Sorry. Probably not a favourite topic for a first date. Or ever.

We can roll around on the grass for a bit to lighten things.
If you'd like.

Faces turned to each other. His stubble like lazy stitching.
That's a good idea.

That was the first time he heard about my brother.

Slowly, slowly. Who needs the details?
                    He knew there was trouble.
                    For a while, that could be enough.

All day John hesitates
the corners of his eyes keep lookout

I stop myself from hissing
                    I imagine I am a goose,
                    throat wide and tongue rippling

                              agitated

it's inevitable
we have company   brother like cotton wool,
                                   stuffed in my head

How was your night last night?
I attempt to regain something.
It's what I would have asked this morning, after all,

him turned to sober
that time in bed before anything has begun.

Fun, yeah. They were on good form.
He plays along.
*Mike's got a new girlfriend and seems to have simultaneously
developed a taste for theatre. Jack's as Jack as ever.
They both asked after you.*

That's nice of them.

*To be honest, I just wish I had been at home.
I hate that I wasn't here.*

It's fine, really, how could you have known?

How are you doing?

I'm okay.
The words a success.
Building bricks.

It's a lot, he says.

Breath like a hiccup. Yes, it is.

It still doesn't make any sense to me, I say
*I cannot reason any of it. How he—
I can't make it fit into easy statements.*

Him, or him having died
                I'm not even sure which one I mean

                I hardly think of the farm I used to work on
that's what I should say
when I was fourteen, fifteen,
collecting eggs and cleaning the sides of the troughs
it was the centre of my week
but now I hardly remember

I've told him parts
                        how I would catch Mr Skinner
                        scrubbing the edges I had missed
                        or taking the shearer out of my hand
                        and saying No, love, try it like this.

I was there every week yet now   it's compressed

I'd spend time dissecting what my nose picked up
                        sharp pesticide
                        shit turned in hay

I wanted to be there precisely because they wanted me,
that's what I remember, Mrs Skinner offered me tea
(pretending I liked tea until magically one day I did)
eating drop scones with home-churned cream
it was as if I had entered a daydream
a half-baked imagining of what family life could be

the two sons would lazily cross their arms, backs against the
stove, and tease their mum until she would shout somehow
sunnily

YOU CAN BUTTER THESE YOURSELVES,
YOU KNOW.

They welcomed me out of what seemed love but now seems
clearly pity, sending me home with eggs in cardboard, paying
for odd jobs and then to serve at their entrance shop, being
called dear, asking after Dad but never my brother

When I stopped eating meat they made omelettes for lunch
laughed at how their farm practice had changed me
(once I started to see what I did not want to see)

I know the story I should tell   edging around
                 pathetic the way we dance, circling a spot
                 the intensity of it too much to dart towards
                 instead, slowly luring myself in

I told Dad: I don't want to eat meat any more
and my brother smiled
Oh, she doesn't want to eat meat any more!
But nothing more
        which was suspicious

Dad understood,   we rarely ate together
he worked late so often it hardly mattered

but it was bad timing
my brother had recently discovered *The Godfather*
he would play the scene with the horse's head
finding it on YouTube and leaving it on repeat
the scream, the silken red sheet, going on and on and on
his hand hard against my sternum
flat, like a traffic controller if I tried to turn it off.

One morning
there were four slices of bacon on my pillow,
overlapping with a wisp of my hair,
their grease leaving shadows.

I knew he would be listening
so I didn't scream
it would be defeat
I knew that instinctively
as I saw bacon, my mouth tensing shut

I pulled my head from the pillow, twisting my neck,
delicately shifting as if the bacon were asleep.

Pathetic, I remember thinking, pathetic!
You could only manage a bit of bacon! shouting it repeatedly
in my head in case he could somehow hear.
That's nothing, I thought in my head, pathetic, I thought
in my head, as I pulled the duvet off the bed, checking for
anything else, stripping the sheets, nothing, bacon,
is that really the best you've got?

Somehow he had managed to creep in here at night
leaning close to my face while I slept
I thought about that as I washed my hair, hands hidden by
foam, thinking about it still

              him right by me, smirking as he rested bacon
              gently, intimately, by my face
              close enough for my breath to warm it
thinking about it still, as I threw up bile, folded on the
shower floor, streaking the soap with yellow, water hard
against the base of my back
I couldn't even sleep in this house without being afraid.

                      He denied it, of course
                      hands on heart in actorly hurt
                      when I said,
                      as casually as I could deliver
                      Next time, at least cook it first.

                      That imagination, he said,
                      you should put it to better use.

Too late now   if I say it
reduces   bubbled to nothing   not nothing,   stupid!
waving slices of bacon   in the face of death
                             never enough
sieving for examples but what does any of it prove

even if it works   if it is something
then   how am I allowed to grieve

how am I allowed to grieve when   part of me

part of me feels   jesus

John's face is open and shut
sympathetic but confused
                                        studying me   leaving space
as he waits

I can't tell it right
'My brother died in a car crash' is something to say
is something I have already said
but I thought his death, that ending, would make all of this
possible to recount
yet still he is caught in motion   undigested

what is unsaid still is the No, is the please don't say sorry
no one else was hurt   it's conflicted
a small part of me   larger than could ever be forgivable
feels relief

I do not say it

                    I do not say

                    that

                    I wished
                    silently

for my brother to die

and now

he is dead

I do not say,

        I had been waiting for him to die.
        Not willing it, but patient, open, ready.

I had anticipated closure.
It would be a way of uncomplicating.
He would be dead; I would have felt, and I would be done.

There must be a part of me that mourns my brother

how can I tell this story?

      how to translate?

what if that is irrelevant?

what if   simply   I do not want to

Sorry, *I'm okay,*   I say   *dealing with the aftershock.*
The ash in the air.

You could hate your brother and it would still make sense to
grieve, Ro.
He's your brother.

the eternal staggered chorus
        (he's your brother!)

                                        (he's your brother!)
I could tell John   what I can   yes
but I hear the half-phrases

spat in my eyes

                        intimidated me

fingernails grown into weapons

        Alice   his girlfriend

when looked at by someone else, they undo
even when I attempt to, when I scrutinise,
I see a shoebox filled with the memories
John would open   and   each would float out, light!

accounting for little

when looked at by someone else, they're nothing
not just nothing: incomplete
(pathetic)
the stories we tell ourselves don't matter to other people
I don't think I have ever really realised that before

they don't matter

I am not scared of my brother, not now

he's not a ghost

even before he died   he was a lingering memory

I do not wait
          shut down
not today

I used to be well practised
home from school
brother soon here, no longer somewhere
and I would sit on my bed
turning myself concrete.

We had been to London   seen the men painted silver
eyebrows crusting

I would think of them and command my skin to stiff
not permitting even a wrinkle of the nose
and I would wait

to see whether the front door would go

to see how my evening would play out

either, it would be footsteps without direction
or,   the door would sound loud back into its latch

and I would be launched
by what should have been a routine noise: door closed
into action

time to unfreeze, to fold up under the bed
I would try to stay calm (it's just your brother after all)
as I crawled behind boxes I never looked at but knew not to
move   fitting myself into that familiar slot
and I would return to still, silver, not moving a twitch
                    (it was my job not to move a twitch)
lying there (still), schoolbag against my stomach, keys dropped
to the bottom, shoes on, all traces kept to my body, leaving no
trail.

It wasn't just the being hurt that I feared, it was the endlessness
of it, so much of the evening left, how inevitably it would
become a saga, how I would scream pointlessly, that he
would be angry without purpose or conclusion, that it might
be mind games or he might pin me against the floor and
punch me, I couldn't say, wouldn't be able to predict which
way it would go, and somehow it was destined to be my
fault, all while time would pass and we would find no way
of settling it or him, just us misfiring without break without
end without rest, unable to be peacefully in the same place
but often my defence worked
under the bed seemed an obvious place to hide

but the trick was in the stillness, in being silver

sometimes he would go out after that, no sign of me, but not
always

I would stay under, waiting
imagining   to fill my head   what Alice was doing
I would go slowly, no skipping, taking her through the front
door, shoes off, readjusting her hairband,
slowly
                        chatting to her mum in the kitchen
                        who always sat on the same battered chair
                        cigarettes like an IV drip,
                        constant, keeping her going,
                        a pack safe under her left hand.

Sometimes I would turn her mum mean, telling Alice she
looked a mess, like no daughter of hers. I'd extend and
extend, taking it further, harsher, screwed-up face
Alice's mum was lovely, gravelly, warm as cigarette smoke
but my head would make of her someone else.

It made me less alone, if Alice was tormented too
both of us together (separate)
white collared shirts and grey skirts
leaving each other after school but remaining united
weird, mirrored unhappiness   even if hers was imagined

different later   that was never what I had wanted.

I only liked to pretend
as if my brother⠀⠀and her mother⠀⠀were our joint secrets.

I would see her every morning on the bus and it was easier
to deceive, pretending she was too, that we were both
restraining, both stable despite it all
⠀⠀⠀⠀⠀⠀⠀⠀⠀⠀⠀⠀⠀⠀⠀⠀⠀⠀that is what I had wanted

but⠀⠀⠀⠀⠀⠀⠀⠀had I not caused it?⠀⠀⠀⠀⠀⠀didn't I?
with those nights of careful world-building, step after step
taking Alice to the kitchen, mother mouth opening, filthy
fucking slut, all that

she was his when it started, my brother's,
Alice fucking my fucking brother

suddenly he was out
seeing her, staying at hers.

Inexplicable, even then. At home, trying to imagine them
but finding it impossible, impossible to construct: what
would they talk about? how could he measure up to her?
what was it for them to be natural in each other's company?
So much of my mind was focused on the impossibility, the
unrealness of them together
I never considered that I was lucky
that she was protecting me without even meaning to

but what from

what was she protecting me from?
what would he have done if I had stayed on the bed?
if he had ever found me?

                  I prepared for it, feared it,
                  came up with a whole world,
                  a whole routine just in case,
                  but never
never imagining beyond   never imagining if

I used to be so sure

moments, I was not quick enough

then, I was proved right   that, then,
                was what I was waiting for
but what was that? what, waiting to be needled, shoved,
made the receptacle for whatever he couldn't deal with,
couldn't get out of himself, just his anger, his relentless anger,
that was what he wanted me for, what I waited to be used
for, some dartboard, punchbag, something that would take
his hurt, give him power, yes isn't it all so neat, so obvious

but it can't have been like that every time   it wouldn't have

how much was I protecting myself from my brother
and how much was I protecting myself from a fear
light switch off, cupboards closed, under the bed
waiting to begin my evening

it was a ritual
what did any of it have to do with him?

Listen to yourself
a death brings everything alive

A man sits on his bed, alone, hungry.
It is 2 p.m., the worst time for hunger
but there is nothing in the fridge
so he sits, picking at his toes.

Picking at his toes, he thinks.
His thoughts are not constructive, not at first.
He thinks: I am so hungry I could eat a horse.
He thinks: I am so hungry I could eat a house.
Then he hears footsteps outside his door, his sister walking
to the kitchen, and he thinks, again:
I am so hungry I could eat a house.
Something flicks, glints. Not a switch, no, it's subtler than that.
It's like he has turned his head and seen something at the
frame of his vision.
Then, he thinks: I am so hungry I could eat a housemate.

Launching into fairy tale.
What is this?
Should recall it properly. Kitchen. Sitting by the door.
I was only young. Eleven.
Is that right? Was I really?
Kitchen. Rope, wrench, socks.

He moved with a directness that scared me

approaching rapidly, rope around wrists, screaming, he
guessed I would, socks in mouth, trying to spit out, stuttered
choking, resisting as he tied me to the chair, fast, pushing the
wrench against my cheek, fear taming while adrenaline sent
my feet rebounding, as if the floor pulsed with electric

> Don't do this
> It wasn't like that
> it wasn't like that at all
> it was a game

I said I could escape any situation
He proved I couldn't

> it was a game

the collarbone is very easy to break
some babies are born with broken collarbones
just from the exertion of getting out.

Do you want a cup of tea?
John's voice summons me back to my blinking cursor
Please.   I am supposed to be compiling a list
that's my plan

details of my brother   measuring my thoughts
but   so far   I haven't extracted him from my head

I divert
by reading a Twitter thread
about a dog apocalypse.

In Lewisham, residents became certain that a disease was
killing their dogs.
Barney was only one year old, Deb says. And now he's dead.
Vomit all over the floor. It happened to her neighbour too,
dead in the garden. The dog, not the neighbour. And two
doors down across the road. Dead.

The revelation
thirteen tweets in
is that someone was leaving out poisoned ham
laced with pesticide, maybe.

Two weeks before the Lewisham apocalypse, a man called
Graham Hann had posted in the neighbourhood Facebook
group

17:02
WILL YOU ALL LEARN TO
KEEP YOUR DOGS ON LEADS

17:11
I AM FED UP OF GETTING
SALIVA ON MY TROUSERS

Here you go, John says.

Tea by my arm.
Thank you I'm okay   answering the question yet to be asked
just   a bit   spaced out.

He stands behind me
brushes his knuckles against my cheekbone
like he's polishing shoes
before kissing where my hair parts.

I don't learn much from Graham Hann's Facebook profile.
He's staring at the camera, and in one picture
his red checked shirt is only half tucked in

an interruption of stomach where the flap pokes up

I don't laugh at how much Hann looks like ham, but I
certainly smirk

I drink my tea and close my tabs
open my list
so far, I have one item

**My brother spat in both my eyes, then pushed his thumbs
into my lids to keep the spit in**

not much of a story
more, a lingering sensation

making me connect things

John, slamming a cupboard door   me, neck reared back
                                  ears twitching like prey
                                  ready for what comes next

if nothing happens
that doesn't release the tension
I'm still expecting

I had forgotten how alive my body is in these moments
                              every limb linked, ready.

Some facts are more helpful for embellishing a story
other things happened,
but the spit in the eye is visceral   gives what it needs to give

an easy first on the list, a well-learnt line

I repeat it when I need to explain
when I have been asked,
                DO YOU SEE YOUR BROTHER OFTEN?

I follow the same emphasis, beginning:
Well, let me tell you a story.

Tried it once, with brother out of shot   (I thought)
                Well let me tell *you* a story,
                he said, head spinning round.

I swear I heard his neck crack

                She set my fucking hair on fire!

everyone likes to exaggerate.

Do take a biscuit, John says.
Okay, I say, knowing I should smile   give a facial cue

I do remember

        A woman near the exit with a paper plate
        Do take a biscuit!

I know

That's what I'm sure she said, Do take a biscuit!, but I repeated
it so many times afterwards that I can't know for sure.

        I don't want this, I said, when I was out of the
        cinema, into the air, disorientated by how light it
        was, the low sun still brighter than I had expected

        I held the Jammie Dodger in my palm, face up.
        Why did you take it then? John said,
        almost under his breath.
        Because she said DO TAKE A BISCUIT!
        Do kill a man! Do lick the pavement!
        Oh fuck off.
        He poked me then

Do still love me!
Fine, I said, but only if you DO eat a biscuit.
His lips were wide on my palm like a fish
Sorted, he said, or tried to say, with a busy mouth.

Since then, biscuits have been accompanied by a verbal curtsy
knowing wink
but today, it's harder

You know you're my number-one priority, yeah?
              John's hands against the curve of my neck
              yes, this
Where's that coming from?
Tomorrow, the conference, I just want to make it clear,
I'm going to bail: it's no hassle.
John. You need to go. This is massive. You're doing the keynote.
You're ... This is life stuff. There's infinite time for me to be sad,
this is a one-moment thing.
No, it's not, I don't care.
Yes you do, and you should. You can't be the replacement speaker
and then cancel in turn. It's too important. Besides, Erika the
Great is going to be there, you mentalist, you've been going on
about that for long enough.
We can reschedule.
Because she's always over from the States isn't she, and your
chapter doesn't depend on her. Don't do me the disservice of
thinking you can get away with saying it doesn't matter. I'm
fine, honestly, if you were away for a week, a month, I would feel
differently, but you're not—

John's face moves, fleetingly
like something has travelled over it
pushing it on

Are you sure?
One hundred per cent. I couldn't live with myself if you didn't
give your talk, if I was the reason . . . It's just, no. And you'll be
back Monday morning, and we can talk about stuff and you can
give me a million hugs.
Three million hugs at least. I can try and come back sooner. I'm
speaking to Erika on Sunday afternoon, keynote Friday night,
the rest doesn't matter. Not really. And once I'm there I can try
and find an earlier time with Erika.
Have the time you need. I mean it, I'll be just fine.

We exist, carefully, in the present
following the day as if it is infinite
as if this is always where we will be

it is a fantasy I lean into   suspended

                             this is where I am
                             this is where I will always be
I think it   this is where I am
as my phone lights up

Mum calling   this is where I am

I watch it silently ring   this is where I will always be.

Behind a lit screen is a person   elsewhere   waiting

John is oblivious
while I witness my phone convert from call to missed
and look back at my laptop
as if I was only distracted in thought.

To go back a day
just one day
and be held there

as the giant of the school corridors
those looks and look-aways when you pass
yesterday   to be held there
otherwise a day I'd hardly remember   (before the evening, yes,
                                        chopping onion,
                                        Dad, on the phone,
yesterday   before then)
warm kiss in bed then forcing myself up, work at school,
couple of drinks with Sarah. Ordinary, is all.
Reading to Margo
that was something   I could be held there, couldn't I?
I'd pick bed first, next to John, not sure yet what day it was,
eyes resistant to opening
but if not then   then Margo

Is goldfish like cod-liver? she had asked, pausing from reading
                    to look up from the page.

Where on earth did you get that from?
Cod-liver? I prompted
I can see 'goldfish',   I said, tapping the word.

Mum says I need them.

They're beautiful, I told her, cod-liver.
Have you noticed? Like amber.
It's a precious stone   (always having to adjust or expand)
something you might find in a princess's tiara or a knight's
sword, encrusted on the handle   that's what it's like
I've always suspected cod-liver contains secret magic.

Jamie doesn't have to take them.

You and your brother are different people, aren't you, silly?
I had hoped to make her smile but she frowned
Jamie,   she said,
says they stop me being dumb.

Jamie,   I said,   then paused
                        Having to be careful. Not good at that.
                        Not instinctive, anyway.
                        Conscious effort.
Saying instead,
Jamie is wrong about that.

Why do you teach me then?   Smart, Margo. Quick.

72

Because not everyone learns the same way, Margo.
And we have fun, right?

She screws up her face . . . Yes.

Then there we go. Maybe we just do it because we like to.
I don't read with Jamie, do I?
Maybe you're the special one. I nudge her arm.
Too far. Sarah would stay Stop, stop, stop.
Too personal, and too specific.
But it made things better, didn't it.
                          She perked up.
                          Read me three pages from that book.
It worked.

Yes, that is where I would go back. Just a little more delay.
Walk through the corridors with extra bounce
order a bonus pint in the pub
linger, luxuriate   in the everydayness of it all

(I wouldn't though, would I?
because the extra bounce, pint, life,
would only be if I knew that I was escaping, avoiding, delaying
and if I knew that   I wouldn't be   escaping, avoiding, delaying
it would be hanging there   I'd be carrying it with me
slowing me to the mud-trudge of a dream) (nightmare surely)

impossible to go back and get anything from it
(impossible too to go back, haven't learnt time travel,

like rejecting something unoffered, but regardless,
though no suggestion it could be mine,

                              no thank you)

instead, only more returning,   how I had said
                                        I'll leave you to it.
Nervous as I spoke.
Brother soon home for the day
                    first time since he'd started his job

    what was I, sixteen?   seventeen?

I had said,   I'll leave you to it
Promised I'd see Ash, I told Dad.
Did you now.
Yes. Besides. Good to leave you guys to catch up. Men
things, lads who lunch, all that.
Rosa, you are staying right here.
No I'm not, and you'll prefer it this way. We'll only claw at
each other, turn it into something horrible.

Dad held his forehead with one hand
                    like he was checking it was still there.
What did I do, he said, to make you two like this . . .
To make it impossible to even have you both in the same
room?

You did nothing, Dad. Just.   It'll be better this way.

And out I went. Not really meeting Ash. No one wanted to
talk about anything other than Alice then. Sent me in the
opposite direction. Didn't want that so no, I wasn't meeting
Ash.
What would I have done, walked into town?
That would have felt appropriate.
Taken up time, yes, I must have done.

I remember The George, at least.
Ushering my successfully ordered pint into the corner,
settling in a high-backed booth with my book
I was reading something that took me away   fully lost
it was around then that I had begun to make my way
through Daphne du Maurier but it was *Jamaica Inn*, I know,
that delight of being in the pub as I read

the novel's mugs of ale similar to my beer in its handled glass
raising to my lips almost absent-mindedly   almost
that paperback like a Reserved sign whenever I returned to
the bar

until three pints and a pack of Twiglets in, I was less reading
than theoretically observing the practice of reading, turning
pages, encountering words, knowing that tomorrow I would
be leafing back to what I really remembered
but that not mattering   all of that was enough

it was a trial   a test to see whether it would be possible
whether I could   simply   say no to seeing my brother

the answer   magic, hoppy on my tongue
was that it wasn't just possible
it was thrilling

I cherished that day   texture still nostalgic
a moment where I was only myself
alone, not hiding from the fact of my brother
only choosing something else and feeling okay
better than that: bold, strong
despite the new reality of Alice, still, I knew I was okay
even though I got back to Dad, late
sunk into the sofa like a collapsed cake
watching a football match, I don't know what, not now
as I slid down next to him,
                                    leaning my head against his shoulder
There you are, he had said
with a plainness that had encouraged me to keep on at the
screen, as if fascinated not turning, while my eyes burned.

Sudden thump again,
another knock on the door, another someone ignoring the
doorbell

can that door have a day off?
How many times today has someone been at it, wanting
something
as if there's a rumour it has been blessed
as if they all know it was where my brother, weeks ago, was

hovering

Pizza,   John says, answering my unspoken question
           of course, right, that makes sense
Thanks, I say   as he scoots up
dancing down the stairs   feet over-emphasising his path
           saying I'm on my way!
           Don't go! I'll be there soon!

Piiiii-zah   back
smell already hitting   *Oh yes please.*
Do you want a beer with it?
My soulmate.   Parking pizza by my side.

Palm on top, I close my eyes
      hearing the jangling contents of the fridge door
heat under
if I brought my hand to my nose   it would smell doughy
          already

Here you go   distinct hiss
Exactly what I want right now.
Say if there's anything else?

Moving down
crossing my legs on the carpet,
two pizza boxes spread side by side
I've got just what I need right here

stay within this   I do

even when I realise
                                        back of head
insisting itself forward

it must be twenty-four hours now
one whole day since I heard

but no, stay within this
not   that fever so intense I began to see mice
not   how they tried to drag my fingers from me with their
       teeth, burrow under my calves
       I would wake up screaming and hear my dad groan
           NOT THOSE FUCKING MICE

John takes my hand between both of his, rubbing as if I'm cold.

                    knew I was better when the mice left
                    leaving my brother in their place
Tell me, John says, *what's going on in that head?*

Oh   I try to be both honest and unspecific,
some thinking
some things I haven't thought about in a while.

I had that when Dad died,   John says, studying our hands
like certain memories had been locked shut
suddenly   there they were.

Like what?   I ask him.

He hasn't said this before, yet he speaks casually, as if not
mentioning it had never been a fixed choice, just how it was.

Hmm, he says. *Like what. Well you won't like this one.*
Go on.
Literally the day after he died, I remembered my sixteenth birthday.
He sent me an email   *subject line: Happy Birthday*
in the body of the email was just a link to Pornhub.
What the fuck?
Yeah, I mean, obviously I knew about Pornhub already,
it wasn't exactly news but like, what was that?
What did you do?
Nothing. Nothing. I didn't reply! I didn't mention it. I forgot, or
I made myself forget. It was only the fucking day after he died
that I remembered. And even then, I wasn't sure. I don't know.
How did I know my brain wasn't fucking with me? I actually
logged in to my old email, my Hotmail, and searched for it. And
there he was.
Oh, love. That's grim. Why didn't you say anything?
I didn't want to.
I nod once,
twice.
What I'm trying to say, via Pornhub, is that I'm here for you.
To listen, to anything:
to distract, to hug   he pulls me in.
I don't say: But you're leaving tomorrow.

I close my eyes and press on the back of his hand
Love you, I say instead, *I love you.*

Friday

Sometimes, still, a glimpse of John will return him to that
first time
a glint really,   there   then gone
                         for a moment   a stranger again
back to that one look which couldn't trade on anything,
not even his voice, no whispered summary from a friend

                    only the bareness of sight

then and now   both   gorgeous

              yet far apart, different

one intimately mine,   one spun in the wonder of anonymity

it was at a friend's party when   looking to the side
I caught him in a mirror

He was in profile, the light bleaching his hair,
and I studied him
this man I had not yet met
but who was so nice to look at already
and as I studied him, he turned his face and met my eyes
                                        still in the mirror

It's strange, the difference.
If we had made eye contact across the room
my eyes would have continued to travel, ready to take in more,
only retrospectively thinking,   hello? was he? do I?

Instead, our eyes caught   and held—

We looked. Continuing to look. And in continuing, the
decision was made – keep on! – so we kept on. Looking.
Looking. Looking, until I sensed my mouth stopping itself
from stirring.
I recognised it in him too: grinning without needing to grin.

The speech continued and we continued, on the brink
of laughing but holding back. I felt like I knew this man
already, the mirror making him both near and far, him
entirely new, yet, contact still, I could have known him for
ever, have been in this moment for ever, I'm sure I felt that
then, looking, and picking up an essence of him, something
in that look, him, that I still see.

When the speech was over, everyone laughed
a party hijacked by drunken spiel

but within my laugh was more
                                          glee at something that was nothing yet

we didn't introduce ourselves, not straight away,
someone turning to me afterwards, drinks, the distraction of
being back to before

but I knew where he was in that room, and I grew restless,
so much of my head tracking him, imagining him, still
locked in that look.

I went to the kitchen to get another drink, hoping that my
movement would trigger his own, hoping he was doing the
same, tracking, waiting, wondering, too distracted by our
new focus to talk

he would only disappoint once we spoke, I warned myself
away from expectation, waiting to be disappointed, making my
way to the kitchen, still waiting to be disappointed, (hoping
not to be), (sure I could not be), still telling myself, you'll only
be disappointed, when I heard someone behind me say

                                                        Hey.

That was it: hey

I turned around and he said

Hey,   again   then laughed
That's as far as I planned, he said.

edges of his mouth,

hinting

Hey,   I said.

Then
neither of us saying anything at all
                        looking as if we were back in the mirror

waiting for what was next

> Shall we get a drink?
> There's a pub on the corner.

Surely there must have been something in between,
but that's what I remember: Shall we get a drink?

Yes, I said. Now. Before someone else
decides to give a speech.

We sat at the only free table, two stools touching, talking
through the dense air   through people shrieking
(close to ears) each in turn reinforcing the need for the next
to shout.

We were able to understand each other, just, the sound
making silence impossible, there could be no awkward delay,
something was always rushing, roaring, it seemed like we
were pitted against the pub

not an annoyance; it united us.

It was only when we went for a cigarette that I realised we
didn't know each other's names, two drinks down and having
clicked into place as if we already knew, that mirror like a
first meeting, but of course we didn't, and he laughed as he
learnt mine, resting against the pub wall, the air chill, him
close, saying it again and again, breath like smoke, as if he

had something that belonged to me, Rosa, he said, me close
to his mouth as he said it, Rosa.

I had never believed it   that someone could fall for me like that.
Always knew I could, would, no surprise there, no
but for him to look back at me like that
                    Rosa, he said.
                    I heard my name like someone else.

What a lesson
a miracle
that was how it felt   still does

to wake up   like this   for this to be more
for it to be   always   something

                              halo of warmth around him
                              bringing me into it too
arm close against my stomach
                    it could be a morning like any other
                    could be any morning, any morning
                                        any day
the same thing
of him, cosy gratitude, yes all that except this morning
something   disconnected   feeling it almost
                                        theoretically

the radio frames our surroundings   like a musical moat
as we lie   silent   in the warmth of bed

as he rubs my arm to say   I'm here

How are you doing?   he asks

Tired,   I say
busy mind.

Eyelids still flickering in and out of the morning
                              heavy, sticky, unsure.

Time, I say
for you to speak me to someplace else,
go on, I say
distract me. Tell me about your keynote.

A demanding start to the day, he says,
hand on my stomach
talking into my neck.

Pretend like I'm an interested novice on Stein,
which I guess I am.

Alright, let me shuffle my papers, he says,
patiently playing my game
one of the interesting complications . . . with Gertrude Stein . . .
is what she didn't acknowledge, he says.
I'm hooked, go on.
Oh believe me, I will, he says.
What's interesting, are the gaps in her writing

and in how she spoke about herself,
after she died, her partner told an interviewer that Gertrude
hated her own past, barely liked to talk about it. Referred to it
as little as possible. I think it was easier then, to do that. Makes
me think of Bob Dylan, James Baldwin, that thing of being able
to fuck off somewhere, the possibility of remaking yourself and
leaving no prints. It's still possible now, of course, but you could
hide more then, maybe.

She must have thought about it though, I say,
her past, where she came from, that she was Jewish, all that.
Yeah, she must have. You can't just bury everything. She said once
'What is the use in remembering anything?' but that resistance
was her limitation, I think it is anyway,
an interesting exercise sure but it could have the wrong motivation

        rolling over to face him
        he speaks gently
        correcting his body to fit mine

to say, again and again, 'I'm not bothered',
only means 'I care greatly', surely?

        hand in my hair, fingers split apart
        brushing against my scalp
        nothing to heal yet   healing

Rosa,   he says
I don't have to go.

I had been waiting for him to say   I don't have to go
I had my response planned.
This time, I would not say go.
This time, I would say, Really? I would say, I know it's a big
deal, you're a superstar to have been asked to step in,
I know it's important, I know you've been working on it for
weeks, and yes Erika will be there, yes your book needs this,
but I think, if you go, I would say, I will go mad, or die,
or something I can't come up with yet,
so yes, I planned to say, please stay.

Except   now he has said it
(I don't have to go.)

the response doesn't feel right.
He half-looks at the bedroom wall, flicking from it to me
protecting me from his face.

He is ready to stay   yet
                        has perspective
that is what the flick tells me
flick to my eyes, I love you, flick to the wall, but I could go

something in that   in his divide
in his empathy that exists in context
                (something else allowed to be important too)
makes things seem okay

I do not say   stay please stay

Instead,   *Go, I meant it yesterday*
                  and I mean it now. I'll be fine,
                  it's only a few days,
                  and he was my brother   yes,
                  but you know how things were,
                  I'll be okay.

                  It's only a few days, he says.
                  Flash of lightning, I say.

                  Blink and I'll be back, he says.

I blink, opening again. *There you are*
                        just like you said.

How must he see this?
kept from what happened

it had been simpler
not to mention
not to say   my brother turned up at our flat.

To say,   my brother turned up
was to say   I dismissed him.

Unable to deliver the missive harmlessly
I knew that   know that still
I would have looked heartless
I knew that

could see it   the decision was bound in silence
                       to be done and then forgotten

otherwise   the disappointment in his face
yes I didn't need to say to imagine

You didn't even let him in?
You didn't even give him a chance to voice what he had
come all the way to say?

                       gifting him the questions
                       I don't ask of myself

never really knowing, never allowing

maybe,   he'd understand

                       placing lines in other people's mouths
                       but mine
I made them,
shaping before executing with another's tone   inside my head
chorus   yet   all of it is me
conversations I have played out   only ever drafts

I lean out of the warmth   to reach the time on the radio
It's somehow ten o'clock.
Well, if I am going, I am going to need to get up.
Get out of bed this instant.
Alright, he says   planting a kiss on my forehead as he goes.

                         He's a dick, Alice.
That was the closest I ever got
her eyes trained on me while she checked how serious I was
before ignoring anyway   He has a dick, she said,
                         tongue poking out of her mouth.
                         Ew. No.
                         Yes.
                         Fine. But no,
                         not what I was saying though.

                         Maybe he fancies you.
                         Alice!
                         What? You couldn't blame him
                         if he did.
Shoved her. Bit too hard, probably.

Being a teenager a second time would be so much easier

you'd know what to take seriously and what to laugh through
how to push back

I don't think I would have unbuttoned my shirt
one science lesson, when a moron at the back had insisted
(while only asking)
Alice next to me, two buttons down,
done in haste yet without moving shoulders
race of subtlety to not let the teacher notice.

But I did

my boobs bigger than Alice's, bigger than most then
and Moron's mate had slapped his hand on the table
shock of real flesh in front of him
what he had only seen so far online
before looking down and seeing Moron's lap
laughing   He's got a bloody boner
I had liked it   in secret   in half measurements
that first jolt of knowing what my body could do.

        Now though, I wouldn't   I wouldn't
        giving him my body
        as if it was what was owed
        them making the rules
        the only way to impress   two buttons, okay
        as if we were part of the game
        when really we were obeying

        I wouldn't do that a second time
        now alongside the jolt is a sickness
        that boys know are taught, shown at that young
        even at school, we were there to supplement, to
        be exploited, enjoyed even at fucking school but
        yes alongside that
        when I don't feel the anger or sickness which is
        most of the time because how can I really keep
        that inside of me,
        so long ago, and so normal, so usual,
        so small really
        schoolboys ranking girls, lacking heart,

that can hardly send me raging when I
remember
and anyway
what about the jolt
             I can still feel it   the startle of my body
             I know I would have learnt it another way I know
but I didn't so I want to keep it

a second time,
                   I'd tell people when I liked them
                   I'd know the effect of saying what I wanted
                   that anyone can inspire feeling
                   I didn't need to like the look of my face or
                   my body or the tone of my own voice to
                   conjure want

a second time,
                   I'd tell my brother enough
                   I'd ask Mum for better

yes, I can think up ideas, sure   home fucking improvements
but   wouldn't it get tiring
the second stint   able to discern
maybe it's better not to know   for it to just be the way.

John holds my waist in a mock slow dance as the stove-pot
steams then sputters
Coffee?   he's relieved, I can tell

The very least I'd expect. must have played out
          the morning
          his own draft
          different to this one

Crumpets too?
You're speaking my language.

He busies himself his sweetness not unusual but still
I sense its weight
John trying to make sure I'm okay while knowing it's not
about asking but being gentle, there, helping buoy my own
positivity and if I want to speak, here he is

watching it play out makes me resist   stop it

I have to be strict sometimes

      army commander
head-salute, get yourself in gear, be nice be nice be nice
Are you looking forward to it? I ask him
         (be nice, be nice, be nice)

Ah, as much as anyone looks forward to stilted conversation and
fridge-cold sandwiches. But it will be good . . . or good to have
done, anyway.

        he takes a bite of his crumpet,
        butter shining on his lips

You're feeling okay about your talk though? You should, you were
sounding sparkling last week.

      strange to think this would have been our focus
      checking he was doing okay before he left
      worried for him without needing to be but still
      checking

Yeah, good, I think. Nervous, but not in a bad way. I'm as
prepared as I can be.

    What was the first thing my brother said, at the door?
    Alright. Leaving me, really, to be the first to speak.
    But were my words any more real than his?

I didn't expect to see you again
              that would have been more real
I didn't want to see you again
              that would have been even better

but even   then   what would that have achieved
I would have had to have spoken something I cannot
imagine now, speaking to get closer to how I felt, what I
would have wanted to say, speaking into that dance again,
always that dance, moving around a point, and in speaking
he too would have returned with the same, together building
something, entering some kind of realm that I cannot
imagine here, that is impossible to explore without him
imagining in halves,   only hypotheticals
now, never going to get close.

Crumpets eaten, coffee drunk, nothing in between
his bag on the kitchen chair
Well, he says
arms towards me.
Make sure to say hi to Christine, I say,
and watch the switch of recognition   eyes blank then alive
laughing harder at the lack of expectation.

Christine both exists and does not

so much of what was real has been written over
her scarf was covering her name badge   so he told me
whenever he was in a room, there she was in the corner

she was christened when we spoke on the phone and he said
There's a woman who will not stop grinning at me, I'll catch
her eye by accident and she gifts me with thirty-two teeth.
Oh, that's Christine,   I replied
I sent her to give you moral support.

And that was it   Christine

I have never asked,
            What does she look like?
                        Where does she work?
                                    What's her real name?
                                            How old is she?

I keep to my imagination

all I know is that at every conference, there she is
we joke that she's obsessed
but she's a punchline, not a threat.

We would return from the pub
and notice a light accidentally left on
Oh god, I'd say, check behind the doors for Christine.

The postman early on a Saturday
when we're still wrapped around each other
For fuck's sake, he'd say, unfurling, dressing gown on
Can't she give us a moment's peace?

I'll start my restraining order application on the train, he says
as he collects his keys, pats his pockets unconsciously,
then consciously.

A kiss, a hug, *Are you sure?*
No, really, go,
and he is gone.

Blink and I'll be back.

It is important in moments like this
to establish a state of being busy
him gone and me
nothing
yes, I must establish a state of being busy

easy at first
I wash up our plates, knock coffee grounds into the food
waste, wipe the surfaces, studying the kitchen slowly,
                              moving

                    jaggedly

                      through

                                to check there is nothing left

only then, do I allow myself to text him
                    Don't forget my name
                    XXX

A joke that's lasted since first meeting
                              since, becoming something else
shorthand   miss you, love you, here I am

I hover over my phone, flicking to last messages
who might be able to distract me
haven't texted anyone since my brother died
not long really

Sarah must have texted minutes before I heard, regretting
we had only stayed for a couple before heading home from
the pub.

There's a reply typed out that I had forgotten

half-written when Dad called
Next time, you need to te

It gives me nothing   I look at it but   can't explain
It has lost meaning   blank

backspacing to the beginning, I try something else
**On the off-chance you're around,
I'm extremely interested in being
distracted.**

I have cake?   before I've even locked my phone

Bring it immediately.

Twenty minutes later, Sarah is at the door. Foil in her hand.

You're a hero, I say. *Can we grab coffee?*
I'll leave this parcel of goodness for when I get home.
Sure, she says, eyeing me.
We don't speak as we walk but she rubs my shoulder and
hums an unfamiliar tune
caught in the fluster of before
                              of something to come
Only sitting down, coffees in front of us,
does she ask the question.
What's wrong?
My mouth turning down in a silent answer.

                              Just say your brother died.
          Sounds bad.   Say it.
My brother crashed his car.   Liar.
          Well it's true, isn't it?

Her face says Oh god. Her mouth says *Is he okay?*
No. Well. He's not anything.
Sob. As if from the centre of the earth.
Pulls me up quick, straight, like marionette strings.
Right through me.

Oh, Rosa. He's?   Nodding.   *I'm so sorry.*
She gets up.   Chair fast scrape.
Don't. It's fine. It's fine. It's fine.
We have an audience. I thought I might be more together
this way. Nervous coffee drinkers,
intent on lift, sip, settle
eyes flicking to us as if by chance

I hear the windows they leave   slow-paced chat
                    for me to fill

First week at Millfields, Sarah made herself present.
We both worked the same window: Mondays to Wednesdays
reading to the kids after lunch before PE.
My day was up but I walked cautiously to the staffroom.
Not sure whether to stay, head, what.
She came in as I stood over a chair,
pretending to be lost in thought

We're going to the pub aren't we, she said,
picking up my coat and putting it in my arms.
She said it as if it was definite. But she held the silence
waiting for my answer rather than ushering me out.
That proved an uncertainty she was trying to hide
she still depended on my answer   was unsure how I'd react.

She could say Pub, putting my coat in my hand
but she was going to wait for the Okay
which I said (Okay), my arm in hers. Where's good?

A Wednesday tradition, our walk to The Ship.
One and a half usually. Enough to calm, catch up, transfer
the week from work to done.

We had stouts this week. Getting cold. The fire was lit and
Sarah had told me how   her cheeks pinking in the heat
recently, on the way home   freckles disappearing
she had bumped into her cat.
Possum, she had said, soft, surprised, and the cat had looked
from side to side, as if embarrassed to be engaging with a
human.

But then he walked home with me.
Well. I think he thought he was walking *me*.
He kept two strides in front and would turn every couple of
minutes to check I knew the way.

That image. I laughed hard enough to put my hand over my mouth. She joined in. Not ideal when even your cat thinks you're thick. Set off again.

I didn't know. Not yet. Few more hours left.
But as I laughed with the ease that a pint in the pub with nothing to do grants you,

                                    my brother was dead
I was waiting, without knowing, to hear.

I have never considered the texture of our conversations
hadn't thought how much was spent laughing
I almost smile now, just to loosen Sarah's face.

She touches my hand, gentle, touch not a hold.

        John. Head slotted onto my shoulder as we sleep.
        Hand in mine as we walk. Never a decision, there.
        Held without question.

Anything you need, Rosa, I'm here.
Is John being good?

Yeah, yeah.
I try to perform what she expects.   Stability,
                                    sorrow set in acceptance
my voice acts like a confession   admitting how I am
I force it out like a ghost
coming out of me but not mine, this does not belong to me

It can't feel real. It won't, not yet
none of him does   like he's   split off
Remember when Margo's dad died?
Jesus, don't I.
I always think of what she said to you
blank space   *What did she say?*
You came out of the classroom and found me
She waits for me to remember, then shakes her head and
carries on
she said to you,
How can I believe he's dead when he hasn't told me?
We grin. *You would think if he had done something as*
important as dying he might keep her informed.
Wise Margo. It feels about right.

     First time I read to Margo, she said:
     Your voice is funny
     Like Mr H has just told you off

     Thanks Margo, I said,
     as if it wasn't the second time I had used her name
     as if I knew her sneaking path to a wind-up
     but I didn't and yes I was scared of a little girl
     with an insistent mouth

You weren't close with him were you?
she grimaces at her own words
Sorry, that sounds insensitive, I'm just half-remembering
something you said before.

No we weren't   though
I wonder how much that helps
so much of my life was in conversation with his
and then, so much fiercely separate.
That's not easy,
she fiddles with the spoon on her saucer.
I didn't mean to lure you into it all,   I say.
What are you talking about?
I said I wanted some distraction
but really I've lured you into a chat about   (can't quite say it)
(I go to be flippant but I can't quite say it)
I'm your friend, Rosa, it's allowed,
more than that, I want to be here for you
I'd be annoyed if I didn't find out until Monday at work,
she pauses
not that you should come in on Monday, might be good to give
yourself some time, take yourself out of all of it.
I'll probably be there. Will be helpful to have somewhere to be.

Knock on my bedroom door
evening Mum was gone
not out, gone
I'll see you at the weekend, I promise.

                              (Didn't.)
                              (Did say it,
                              didn't see us.)

It was a not-quite knock. Enough contact to be heard
but not enough to express trouble

106

fist gentle on the door   noise of skin and wood
then s-tipped hiss   (Sis?)

What is it?
I was sad, irritable,
not partial to a needy brother
heart bent though   by muffled wood

                                            Hug, he said.

Arms still tight by his side
eyes on the verge of my face
not quite looking

You repressed fuck   I wouldn't have said
being too young to know to say that   not quite yet
but looks can go a long way

I could give a hug, sure, did   until he let go,
                                            quick disentangle
                                            as if I'd thumped him

disappearing out the room
                                            Nice to see you too!

only to reappear at speed
crisps in one hand   Game Boy in the other
pillow carried under a rigid arm.

Okay, Sarah says, folding speech in with movement
her chair whining as she stands up

We're going to do something with you.
Threatening, aren't you meant to be sitting in your
pyjamas doing your emails?
Yes, but here we are. We all had visions for our Friday. But it's
also Friday, a day arguably more deserving of being a day of rest
than Sunday.

To be honest, I say, as we leave the café, her arm in mine,
on the precipice of a plan
I'm not sure I'm up for much. I think I just need to go home
and sleep,
and clear my mind,
and eat your cake.

Okay, she says, after studying me to check I mean it
I'm not sure I do
but my face seems to convince her
you promise you'll text me if you need anything?
Course. But really, I'm fine. I'll see you on Monday, okay?
If not before, depending on how you're doing, because you'll tell
me if you need anything.
Yep, blah blah that, exactly.

We hug at my door, and she goes.

Not in yet, watching as she nears the top of the street
unassuming from that far

from a distance, her clothes turned vague
sweatshirt indistinct
high-waisted black of her jeans easy to miss
there she is,
sincerely putting one foot in front of the other
yes, a little funny

she turns
I raise a hand: high, flat, still   in a saluting wave
                                  she matches with energy
                                  spasmed back-and-forth
                                  before the corner swallows
        her
(gone)

not sure why I asked her to leave,
why I wanted to be alone, if I wanted to be alone,
                    or whatever else,
                      however else she read my decision

Reason hardly matters. Done now. Back to me,
back to the flat.

                        Into the flat.

Here you are. Here I am.

Under the foil   a thick slice of banana bread
and a napkin decorated with smiling lemons

                          Delicious, I text Sarah
still chewing my first bite

Underneath, a photo from John, five minutes ago.
I click and feel that tiny lift in my chest, a shot of his legs,
                            crossed at the ankle
still, at the silliest thing, my heart   red scratch of train
                            carpet underneath.

our way of checking in: here he was, alive
the photo meant   I am thinking of you
                            I send one of my hand,
                            pale in the light

his feet are more reassuring than I want them to be
something about him gone
makes me doubt he has ever been here

                            my brother is dead
I know people can disappear into the air
without warning

blink and he'll be back
yet the text is a sign of life

too used to reading into gaps

rather than trusting that the in-between can be a resting place
safe, continuing, reinforcing   not unknown darkness

I know where it comes from   fear in absence

after his dad died, John in the pub after work
almost every night   on his own, maybe, it was hard to tell
I never knew how long he would be
and how I would find him when he got home
so I started cancelling plans, not because of him exactly
I would tell myself I was tired, I needed a break, that I wanted
to be at home which happened to be where I would wait for
him, unable to settle   knowing I was there at least I was there,
I was where he would end up eventually   I would rather have
avoided it   would rather have not been there to witness
but I owed my presence   if I could do nothing else,
I could at least wait

                         it is good that he went   that I said: go
                         otherwise, he would only get the same

it was how I would find him   not how he would find me
deducing what he would push back against, what I could say
without being stared at, eyes dull as if I had caused him to
lose his sight

I have never been very good at dealing with other people
how much of that was him
and how much was me
                         unable to let him grieve how he wanted

I don't know   it was his grief
and it was complicated   his dad was an arse
not in the way some dads are

           the background on his computer was Megan Fox
           at least say something wicked I can bite onto

when I saw his dad,
meet-ups capped by carefully booked trains
I would tilt my chin
pull in the thick of my cheeks with my teeth

if the first test was being enticing
then against myself, I wanted to succeed

                                grey eyes
                                ungiving, flitting

I could tell more from my brother's mouth   always his mouth
thin or turned up, swallowing down or opened wide in a
stretched smile

a month ago on my doorstep
he was softer
hesitant

it confronted me   that softness
reminded me that it had always been impossible to hate
him fully   I couldn't feel anything for him in absolutes.
I had to love him   or at least feel an intensity, an attachment,

an impossible something   connecting me to him   maybe that
is love, yes, and I had to feel it   I resented that, as well as him

but his hesitance   his gentle approach
                                 respectful yet almost
                                 almost desperate
as if he knew it would be the last time

no one knows
not when it's like that

you don't get to prepare a goodbye   a graceful end

you don't get to organise   not if it's like that
can't avoid some trace of comedy

feel out of myself
abandoning phone on the counter   dull thud as it lands

                                 crumpled foil
                                 spiking my hand
        out of myself   no
get this right   trying to pin it down

like I am some gasp of air
inside a body   not mine   detached yet stuck inside   imitation
like the rough crackle of snake skin once it has been shed
whose are these hands?   mine, you idiot

hand slap across the face   igniting life into them   into me
                    yours, you idiot

say it out loud to hear the sound

My hands.

Just talking to myself in the kitchen.

Just having a normal Friday.

Closing my eyes but   rather than nothing,

                  weight   like a vision
                  heavier when I cannot see
claustrophobic to turn inwards, to try and avoid what is around
me, no   not claustrophobic, not exactly
but the weight of my eyelids insists that it doesn't work,
insists that I can't escape
as if it would be so easy

I used to slip into cinematic slideshow
closing my eyes as a kid to   swirls to stars to faces
one face in particular the dark would always turn to
a man who never introduced himself
who would only appear at night
he would have been a fool to enter any other time
when daylight might chip at his menace

unveiling a weak chin

no, he knew what he was doing
waiting for dark, me alone and then
face up close, silent

only disappeared once I had seen him for real

Dad and I going through wedding photos
one last look before he chucked them

(Mum was getting remarried
and it had come as a shock.
I thought he might have realised
when she moved to Leicester
a place she claimed she would never return to
and halted calls after five minutes
because she was simultaneously
too busy
and too cheerful.)

at the end of the album
as the disposables emerged
there was a man near the lens
the flash giving him demon eyes
appearing exactly how he did in my head

I had got him from this photo
it was crude, how closely mimicked

Who's that? I asked
Carefully, neutral
as if the answer didn't matter
I don't know, my dad had said,
it's funny what we forget.

I wash up mugs, keep my hands and legs busy
starving for action
more, more, they demand, so I oblige

peel the bed of its layers
stretching on new sheets
shaking pillows into clean cases

I see us lying here

                how many mornings has my head
                been angled on his chest,
                my shoulder to his centre slightly glazed,
                Pritt-Sticked to each other
                that change after sleep,
                from separate to together
                with a good morning, a kiss, or simply
                a line drawn down his arm with my finger
                in all that   here we are

next, a cup of tea
it's not raining so I carry the mug down the stairs

wrapping my hand tight enough not to drop
                        loose enough not to hurt
twist the latch of the front door
and sit on the top step

I sit
and I watch

at first   nothing happens
but then I tune in

the woman at number 9 cleaning the inside of her window
fast circular motions that I follow until we make eye contact

next, a crisp packet catches under a wheel

music distant, close, then gone

                        everything sifted from my head
            only

        this

a white cat crosses the road and as I stare, straight,
all my energy focusing in on the cat
on its curious arc
                    I think   Come say hi

                    that's it   just COME SAY HI
and he does!
closer, closer
until he wraps once, twice, around my stretched-out leg.
A moment. Those perfect circles looking up at me,
black within green. Like marbles.
Concerned. They can't be. Not really. Just eyes.
Thank you, I say, quietly.
Then I shake my leg
          cat bounds   with paces as long as his stomach

man on the other side of the street   unexpected, there
nods at the cat's escape   then at me   before walking on
herringbone coat cut to the spread of his back
                         a man   that would carry an umbrella
                         steel-capped, long-handled
                         whenever there was a chance of rain
a man I might once have swooned at   not a narrow category
when Alice and I skived school to hitch the train to London
hiding in the toilets as we sensed the inspector
                         waving
                                  their way
                         down the
                                  previous
                         carriage

Alice had borrowed her parents' Oyster cards
so we could beep our way onto the Tube
and sit   in awe   rapture   at the men

I'd turn from one to the next, scattered, admittedly, between
those I'd ignore and wonder   was this being a woman?
surrounded by men and their stubble and their chests like
pillows   that fullness a revelation
                                ready to wrap myself around
                                rest my head against

some holding books, others with palms in laps
                eyes listlessly following movement

                                was this what we had in front of us?

never that now   then, an ideal
            now   men hardly a surprise
so easy to refine   take for granted

that allness of each of them no longer a shock
the foreignness of them, that was how it felt, that there was so
much that they presented, that I knew nothing of yet needed
a language I wanted to learn, that I felt apart from
                                the promise of being invited in
                                        a state of before
            that was what it was then
            yet don't I   yes
            still in awe   stunned   wet
            by my hands across his back   as we fuck
            the manliness   it really is that somehow
            the otherness   the extent of him   yes

but the shock of a Tube carriage   never that again
man after man   each with a different promise
not even capable then of fully imagining what they could do
but wanting it already

Alice had said, as we minded the gap
    walking and swerving up through the heat of underground
That guy was *fit*.
And I had agreed, with a giggle
suppressing the question (which one?)

That was before the year of distance,
before we missed maths in order to scream at each other
Alice insisting I was obsessed with her, I was jealous, I
couldn't handle how she preferred my brother to me

neither of us mentioning what she had said before,
how she couldn't bear the idea of living through the rest of
the school year   let alone everything beyond
that undefinable yet exhausting constant
not just years but a treacly endless ongoingness

we didn't mention that
I screamed other things, that my brother was a cunt, that he
was going to ruin her life just as he was ruining mine, that I
didn't care who she slept with, it was him that was the problem
and that I only wanted my friend back, really, only that

we both calmed and I thought we were going to hug, that
the shouting had been a way of extinguishing what had
pulled her away, I remember it like a thrill, there was hope in
how my voice left my mouth, violence easing our distance

but after we had both looked across at each other, quiet
again, she shook her head

We aren't friends now, she said.

      Disorientating to recall with what came next.
      Otherwise   well   what would it be?
      Would I even remember?
      It would only have been an argument between kids.

It was only an argument between kids
except   I cannot forget
except   I have to relive.

      Never understood
      what she could have felt for him
      how she could have not seen what he was.

Sitting heavy on the step, mug drained of heat
I feel the cold I've been ignoring
                  can't seem to remember how to live

phone lights up in my lap, but I allow myself to look lazily,
slowly,

                                        as if nothing is urgent

                                        which it isn't
                                        not really
only Mum, calling
       her on the other side, listening to the robotic repetitions,

       Hello, I'm afraid your daughter is currently ignoring you.
       Please leave a message after the tone.

She turns to Brian (I can see it!)   almost hear it
Babe, she's still not answering.
He pulls the expression he settles on when something is
expected of him that he cannot give, face spasming as it tries
to find the right setting

I don't hate my mum   I can't

the mother hates the baby before the baby even knows it has
a mother

                                        she's the one who said it

the mother hates the baby before the baby even knows it has
a mother

no story here   only a series of mistakes

Last mistake?

                             Answering the door,
                             only to close it.

I wish I had been out
I wish I didn't know that he tried

it's not that I didn't speak to him
it's that I had the choice

Oi oi   Sarah!   halfway down the street
Sarah!   walking like a cowboy,
                exaggerating her gait as I watch
                self-consciousness becoming goofy performance
Hey, she says, as she gets here,   bottom of the steps,
                                    hands in her pockets,
                                    projecting ease
I just wanted to check you were still doing okay?
Several hours have passed, and the poison in that banana bread
should be having its effect by now.
Ha, ha, ha,   moved that she's here   checking
I'm okay, really. Although I know it's October, and cold, and I'm
sitting on my doorstep, but that's just regular weird me rather
than having-a–breakdown me.
I hoped that was the case. To be fair, I don't really care how you
are. Just wanted to try out that popping-round thing, the whole
Seinfeld–Friends myth of how people see each other in cities.
You fucked it then. Where's your anecdote? You can't enter a scene
without a story.

You're right. You're completely right. Fuck.

We pass a smile between us, happy within that

                                       then her face adjusts

Can I ask you a question?

Okay?

I didn't come here to ask this, but now I am.

Okay . . .

How long do you reckon you'll do reading assistance for?

Our wonderful job that we love very much and that helps heal
divides: spread the word, et cetera?

Yes. That. Our generous, not Christian but certainly godlike job.

I'm not sure. I have no plan of leaving,

in fact   hardly thought of this

the Guardian have asked me   hardly thought

to write a bi-monthly   to think of this

not like, recognisable stories, but a column, a diary-of, that
highlights you know . . . illiteracy, and the success this all has, I
dunno, I haven't fully cracked what I'm going to write about.

As long as it isn't about our Wednesday pub sessions.

I laugh   *Wouldn't make it into print.*

Seriously cool though. When does that start?

Next month. Still need to get school's permission. But I mean, it's
promoting the school in a way, so hopefully they'll be okay.

Yeah.

You're doing so well, Rosa.   *Why are you asking?*

she halts,   I halt,

accidental overlap

I really respect how you juggle the two, she carries on,

and how well it works, you're smashing it.
Thanks. I feel pretty distant from it all right now. Why are you
asking? You're not leaving me?
Silence.
You're LEAVING ME?
repeating my words like a soap-opera diva.
No, no . . . she says, elongated. Not yet anyway, but it's
something I'm thinking about. Loosely. Without doing anything
so far.
Where would you go?
I'd love to work for Solace – or any woman's refuge really.

        Unspoken, not hidden, a nod really
        the night we both said we had been raped
        it wasn't a surprise, just one of those sad
        inevitable matches
        like playing Snap
        if half the cards were the same

        Snap,   pause,   snap, snap, snap

so much simpler with women   often only a verbal nod
it was okay telling John, really
more than that, it helped
continues to
soon after moving in,
him content in what he was doing: reading in a chair by the
window while I sat at the living room table
scrolling   following the drift of my laptop

it was then
I came across the man who had raped me
just like that   no warning.

        Dad would say,
        This is how the world is now
        you couldn't do that once
        now you're confronted with anything

        (not that he knows I was raped
        or would say that if he had just found out
        but different context, yes, he would)

I had told John years before about him
that it had happened, at least
but suddenly here he was, on my screen
I said,   Fuck's sake.
but I had already watched   (muted) the auto-playing video
him on some TV panel, 47 seconds answering a question
I had already watched his face move
hands conducting as he spoke
not thinking anything as I watched letting the video play twice

except   the affront of those hands
how softly they moved through the air

thoughts evacuated   then running back
ushering myself into action
I knew, either I could mention this now

                    (Fuck's sake, I would only need to say)
Or I would have to wait to raise it at a time that seemed
relevant, significant enough to need to bring it up, which
meant more likely I would never speak of it and even though it
didn't matter (not really), I wanted to say, wanted to welcome
him into my head, let him see, I would be keeping something
from him otherwise, even though it was only a video that had
happened to interrupt   nothing more
so I said
                    Fuck's sake.
waiting for him to look up from his book
and reply   What?
for him to see my face and stand up
                        (postcard slipping between pages,
                                leaving it on the chair)
I was grateful not to say it across the room.
When he was behind me, my laptop open
                Introducing my rapist, I said
no, too harsh   too stern
I would have soothed it
have said   Introducing the guy who raped me.
John stood behind me, stroking my arm as I played the video,
unmuted this time
                He sounds like the back end of a plum,
                John said,
                almost under his breath
                but milder than how he felt.

I laughed, cutting short the video

the crown of my head hitting his chest
I wouldn't have been able to say that was what I needed to hear
and maybe it was the fact of him speaking at all
and how likely it was that whatever he said would be right
but it was
it was exactly what it needed to be

I knew my relief was at a cost to him
really, it was worse now, he knew more, had seen his face,
the rapist's face, before, it would have been hazier in the
imagining, more unclear, less real   but now
he knew how he spoke   would recognise him in the street

that meant something, something he could not word, not to me
because it was not his, still
it was mine

while I could pull him into this world and say, here is that
person, here is what happened to me, he didn't have the
same power, not for this, he was suspended
by respect, by caution, to not mention, to only know what I told
him or hinted at, and while I could be as willing or unwilling
as I wanted, he could not admit to the feelings he must have
had, with little control, knowing that another man had raped
me, entered me, gone through with that, knowing that it had
happened, knowing that if they were ever to meet   and
could now, now he knew his face, that John would want to
hurt him, be driven to fucking kill him because that's how I
feel, that is how I would feel if someone had done anything to

John, wanting to fucking tear them apart without even knowing
how or what good it would do but feeling the fury up against
the insides of my skin like I wanted to burst out of myself

furious even at the thought of it, teeth gritting,
even though it couldn't, wouldn't, would be unlikely anyway,
because he's safe, isn't he, no one is safe but he is more safe,
as safe as he could be, and he knows that, all of that, not that
it's something he carries because instead it's the lightness,
I imagine lightness, it must be light to be without knowing
you are being, walking being walking, all safe as it can be

yes I would be furious but it would be less complicated
it would be done to him
me being raped, however intellectualised, there's discomfort,
there's something more invasive, something that travels,
infects others, brings in others,

I don't know how much is imagined, how much real,
knowing that I can never know exactly how he feels because
he cannot say it
He cannot say: I feel uncomfortable that you have been raped.
Difficult to admit that it could be a burden for John too
I understand, can theorise, and yet to hear it, even half-spoken,
my reaction would expand before the words had even landed,
ready to protect myself, the small of his expression growing,
reaching the height I feared, until my reply could only be an
outburst, could only be Fuck you, this is not yours, not yours
to feel, not yours to fucking think about

We hear not what is said but what we fear
deafened by an alternative that has never even played out

no wonder I can't deal with my fucking brother
no wonder.

I'm off to see my sister, she's been threatening to get me drunk, but
I'll see you soon okay?
Alright, have fun. Thanks for coming by.
Lots of love, pal.
Sarah walks backwards, waving, line-drawn smile

I move my hand like a windscreen wiper until she spins round
hand stationed still for a moment
then stiff standing up
back inside, back inside, mug and me back inside.

        Do you never feel like you'll regret it?
        I could have heard John then:
        understood immediately what he meant

That space, where he could have been referring to anything,
anyone.   Like an unwrung sponge.
I didn't want it. Didn't want the heaviness of it. I didn't want
to have to answer the question, not properly, not with the
thought and reflection it needed.

You're going to need to be more specific, I said.
        My mouth closed but curving

                              in the cheeky delay
                              keeping it light
                              keeping to my dance

I could have heard him
known that he meant my brother
but I allowed it to remain vague   just for a spin
for the time it took him to draw more words up
words that had been half-formed, half-phrased   (I knew)
many times before
                              (could hear in the rhythm
                              of how the words fell)

I was resistant   that was obvious,
                                             hardly new
I was resistant   am resistant

In that space   he could have meant anything
He could have meant any of my regrets I never quite allowed
myself yet could summon without hesitation
Yes it was possible that he meant . . .
the cruelty with which I pinned down my mother,
                              strict in her two dimensions
I know where my mind jumps next
John would never have meant it, but in the shadows of that
question
inevitably it stirs
I had never reported him, the man who had crossed a line
                      no,   barricade,

who had raped me that night
like it was as simple as any
other unthinking decision
More stirs, I know, not even beginning to think of Alice,
no, nor what was genuinely behind the question – the
undeniable fact of my brother
solid, real, however much I tried to dissolve him

I could think of so many things I would have or at least could
have done differently at a point when it wasn't too late
shimmering collection of what-ifs   what-could-bes

amazing, really, how many I could tally
if I think that way   if I force myself to
comparing stills   if I were to see it as merely selecting

a)

                              b)

                                                            c)

and later
wishing I had prodded my finger at an alternative letter
yes, that way it does seem simple   foolish
as if life isn't thick with those: a cascade of prods, of yeses and
nos, of silences that can never later be spoken into

sometimes it is as if to regret is to deny the whole thickness,
allness, impossible complexity of the present moment, the
density yet fragility, is that it, yes

where a hand quivering in a lap
      where a sentence falling on the wrong emphasis
         where a love, a care not stressed enough
can set off a chain, a permanence that goes against the
flimsiness of anything committed in the present
what am I saying really other than how terrifyingly alive
liveness is, isn't it that?
The cruelty of having effect, of making impact, of being an
answer or explanation to a moment of someone else's
      the brutality of willing anything into action.

That space   vertiginous delay
Until John said   Your brother, Rosa.
Until he said   I'm not saying you're wrong,
                I'm just poking at it.
                At the severity of it.

There it was   what I could have heard

     instead

Never been so sure of something in my life, I said.
       A lie. I could count a hundred things.
       A thousand.
       Certainty?
       The joke of that.
       The joke of that residing anywhere close
       to my sense of my brother.

It's hard to express, I said,
how much of a relief it is to be clear.

That was half-true, wasn't it?
Playing, pretending at a way of feeling.
But some of it. Some of it was true.

I suspected then that he was challenging a real weakness he
had sighted   like rubbing at a scratch on a table

my background doubt
underneath struggling up   (was I sure?)
questions I had not answered
(was I really that clear?)
(was that possible?)
he encouraged me towards what I had been propelling from
matching poles of magnet
destined or determined to move away
he asked   Do you never feel like you'll regret it?

and I could have heard

he asked it again, later
no, he wasn't done
that time,   he moved beyond gentle gesturing

I had caught him speaking to Dad   not caught, really,
it wasn't that,

134

                              not meant to be

Do you think she'll change her mind, I had heard him ask
as they made tea in Dad's kitchen

hovering   on the way back from the toilet
standing in the space between the stairs and the door
                                        moving not
                                        a single
                                        part of me

I had meant to overhear something sweet,
that had been my plan
John talking about our upcoming holiday, his job,
the fucking weather
I had only wanted to enjoy the evidence of them getting on

I hadn't   wouldn't have paused   if I had known

I had only intended a harmless investigation
ready to be touched at their gentle attempts

instead   something real

        I listened   not agreeing with the action
                objecting   as I carried on listening
                                        carried on,
                                        hardly breathing
I don't know, John, I don't know

you haven't met him, have you?

John saying No, no, not yet   imagining him, then,

                                    slowly shaking his head

                                    thinking beyond

Not ever   I thought   breathing again

                then speaking it   stepping in

Dad, you know I've tried, but I'm done now.

On the train home,   John had asked

                      Are you sure?

and I had known   immediately

                    that we were back on my brother

not indulging the ambiguity this time,

I had said: I don't want to be dramatic.

                  (looking for words that would make impact)

But do you know how impossible it would be,

if you liked him

or didn't mind him,

or couldn't imagine him having done any of it

some of it   anything at all?

                  But I'm on your side, Rosa.

That's not the point, and it's not how it works

you wouldn't need to,

wouldn't need to doubt for me to imagine,
to know you might
that's it, really

I hadn't told him
about the bubbled mark by my brother's temple
that sometimes it felt like what I was concealing about my
brother was really myself
I hadn't told him that alongside fear, frustration, anger
                                        was shame

wasn't there?   shame   for something that wasn't
accidental or overblown or misdirected

No, I had meant it   that was the trouble
I had done exactly what I planned

I could have told John   at least tried to bring him in
                                just a little
so much in my mind will fade
but the puckered yellow skin, that mark on my brother's face,
its subtle difference in how it looked in sunshine or artificial
light, none of that will ever leave me, and I could have told
John, but I didn't

there had been attempts with my brother
there had been attempts and none had worked
apart from   yes   those brief crossovers
when Mum or Dad felt mischievous

as we switched sides at Christmas
misinformation meaning we overlapped   just

Enough to nod at each other a Happy Christmas
him first,
me, Did you enjoy your stay with the rodent?
Oh yes, he would say, great preparation for hanging out with
Doughnut Man.
Rodent would eat him alive, I would say, and watch him laugh
before adding: Probably why Dad got him in the first place.

                              That was easy, wasn't it?

somehow light   despite the gaps   somehow managing

enjoying playing at being related

sibling snapshot   too small for an explosion
                              polite exchange can't be guilty of much.

The day passes   (my brother is dead)
on it goes   (my brother is dead)
but nothing changes
I inhabit the knowledge
I move between rooms
but the plot of my day?   my brother is dead

              the fact dances in my periphery

have I ever seen him dance?

when he was small enough to stand on Mum's toes
but heavy enough that you could see her legs working a
sluggish jive

                                    but if he was small
                                    I was smaller

not a memory
an imagining, surely

I shower as a distraction
reading the back of the shampoo bottle out loud

stopping at   *Silk molecules*

voice unsettling in the quiet
obscuring other noises   not just brother but anything
I am drawing attention, hiding attention

What if I had been in the shower the day my brother visited?
if I had never heard the door

                                    But you did answer,
                                    didn't you?

Shower off,
dry myself using a towel still hinting wet from the morning.
What if I hadn't answered?

> What if you had hugged him?
> Part of you was pleased
> wanted to start over
> finally able to start again.

Mrs Clark was obsessed with forgiveness
I never understood how it could be transporting
whatever she used to chant in English lessons

The resolution of any good story is FORGIVENESS.

She would bang the chalkboard,
her chain bracelet rattling a percussive accompaniment

Without forgiveness, she would insist, a little too breathless,
stories are cold, real artists know forgiveness, know goodness,
their characters are persuaded away from deceit and regret
by opening up.

> Like what, miss?   someone would ask, slyly
> Like *Animal Farm*, miss?
> Have you read that one, Timothy?
> Not yet, miss.   questions make kids shrink
> Oh, miss, or *Cold Comfort Farm*?

her son had just been arrested
on suspicion of slaughtering the Skinners' farm
some of it, anyway:
the pigs, one lamb that I watched learn about its own legs

we knew why she was preaching
why she would sometimes leave the classroom unexpectedly
jaw uncertain

everyone paused after the last question
was it too much? (knowing it was too much)
but then   a giggle   and the whole class ignited
losing it!   some of them shrieking

Should I forgive myself for that laugh? Is that what Mrs
Clark would have wanted? Has Mrs Clark forgiven us? Or
did we make her break her own motto?

I expect to see Mum on my screen
but it's not
it's Dad   jabbing at Accept
                               as if this call could be
                               a reversal of the one before
                               but only if I'm fast enough

I know you didn't speak much

Dad has always been in denial

never able to admit that we didn't speak   at all

but did he ever tell you about his girlfriend?

What? No?

Me neither. She called last night.

Jesus. Who is she?
How long had they been together?

I'm not sure. But they were living together. Julia.
Her name's Julia. She sounded very sweet.
Very, well, I don't know, like a nice person.

Julia   it shouldn't come as a shock

I knew nothing of his life   Does she know, Julia?
most would be guesswork   The kind of person
                             my brother was?

I thought he would be alone   How did he manage it?
I didn't think to consider otherwise
                             Even with Alice, always
                             always, in control.

As we're saying goodbye, Dad asks,
How are you getting on?
and as reflex I say *Great*

then *well*   *no*   *not great*
that would be strange   *to be great.*
He laughs, kindly, a gift for my stumble
You can be anything you want, sweetheart,   he says,
I'm here for you. I can get on a train, just say the word.
Thanks Dad. I'm okay.   I almost believe it as I say so
I'm okay.

I try to imagine what Julia might look like
but nothing

evidently   it is time   to go to the pub
thinking that as a joke, a way of passing the time
but sometimes half-thoughts thought for the sake of thinking
are worth repeating
                    it is time   to go to the pub

let beer seal the cracks

now   now   now,
it is time for the pub
I lock up, head out, streets already stirring for the evening
What day is it?

                                        Friday

Friday
but there'll be space for one

just one

                     Where is she, what is she doing now?
I am borrowing Alice's face   but it's Julia
sweet name, Julia
that's what I would have said
door open, brother there, but not closing it on him
welcoming him up, placing tea in his hand,
the strangeness of him holding something that is mine, too
close, too familiar, as if he should have brought his own mug
yes after that, his feet touching yet knees wide
                           nervous spread
he'd say
                I have a girlfriend now
                we live together
                and her name is Julia

Sweet name, Julia, isn't that what our great-aunt is called?

                Shut up, fatso   he'd say
                tea almost spilling
                as he calms himself.

                Shut up, fatso
                in his silly fake-American flourish.

or maybe   Quit it, fatso.
like it was only ever a joke   yes, that would be it
his favourite   fatso   sharp stab

                              in two syllables
it was lazy: he was borrowing, having witnessed the hurt
but that was all he ever needed

it was Doughnut Man, really, driving us back to the train
station, Mum in the front with him
                              I don't know what prompted it
maybe I spoke, maybe it was only a look
but Mum turned to Brian and said, Silly isn't she, Rosa,
she has nothing to worry about, nothing to complain about,
she's turning into a lovely young woman.
Brian had nodded yes, and at Mum's expectant silence
put the nod into words,
Of course, she's lovely. Could lose a little weight around the
middle, but ...

              but ...

                       even then the scene had a surreal edge,

like fears shown in a dream

on the train back, headphones pressed into my ears
my brother sat diagonally   muted

but I could still see his mouth rounding

              fatso
              fatso

fatso

until I closed my eyes

like the nightmare I hoped it was,
I forgot
(or tried to)

      everything rises eventually

came back in an argument with Mum, years later

Brian was grating, arms around her, not listening, a talker
who waited for a gap or designed one to say what he had
wanted to say two minutes ago.
He disappeared as we began to sharpen our responses.
I said, You only care for your boyfriend, Mum, the rest of us
don't matter.
      (I didn't say husband, if only to annoy her)
Rubbish, she said, not even considering what I was saying.

      Something dislodged.

You once let him tell a fourteen-year-old girl she should lose
weight, for fuck's sake, I said.

      (Brick wall)

What are you talking about? He'd never say that.

The push-and-pull of Yes he did
                       No he wouldn't
                       Well he did!
                       Come on I'd hardly sit
                       there and let him
eventually tired us both out

I felt better afterwards. She hadn't admitted it, but we had
at least agreed that it would not have been fair to say what I
believed he had said and what she believed he had not. The
words, whether his or not, were bad.

                    I didn't think
                    We choose what we want to believe.

Always on her. It was Brian not her who spoke. But I reach
for Mum. Punished for not being there.
                    If it had been Dad,
                       his absence might not have even been noted
                       or at least, it would not be an absence
                       whose outline could somehow still be traced
                       he could simply not be there
But instead, the following-ups, the wiggling-eyebrowed
confusion, the grappling for what kind of woman would
leave a decent man and his two kids, what woman would not
willingly, excessively, give up all of herself for her children
flour on her jeans, kisses on our cheeks, all that caricature, yes

But some of it was there, I know it was, however theoretical

I can be now, the question was always the same underneath, always too easy, it was always, why did she want to leave?

One stout, one table, one man looking at me from the bar

19:07

John must have finished by now

How did it go??

not online since 17:33

back in my pocket, and back to
one man looking at me from the bar
persistent

I make eye contact   hoping it will put him off
I've caught you out,   that's what my eyes say

try to, anyway, but

instead, he picks up his pint, stool drilling against the floor
and steps over, one step,
      two step,
    three step
Nuts?
Excuse me?
Do you want some?
Relief.

Cashews clutched

against the side of his pint.

You're alright thanks.

Can I?   gestures to the chair next to me

surprised by myself,   I do not think: Fuck off

instead   Why not?

which I say   *Why not?*

without considering the question's answer.

My brother died this week   I announce, to set the tone
and today, I find out he has a girlfriend.

Wow, really plunge me into the deep end.
(*And sorry*, he says, face performing sympathy,
about your brother.)
Thank you. It's okay, you see, he was a nightmare.
Oof. He pours a handful of cashews into his palm
then shots it.

Are you going to meet her? The girlfriend?
I hadn't thought about that
yes, maybe, no
the trouble is   *if I do I'll probably end up telling her he's a cunt.*
Might help with the grieving process, hers I mean,
I remember when my uncle died, he says, *my dad told me that he*
had once slapped my mum and it was like some magic pill. I was
distraught then suddenly cured. You could be saving her months
of hassle, if she doesn't already know, mind you, men aren't too

149

selective in their cuntishness.
I think of Alice   *No   I guess they're not.*
Hardly the cheery Friday-night conversation I was hoping for,
no offence   these pints are dangerously low, shall I fix that?
Sure, thanks.
You on the milk stout?
Yes, that's me. Thanks.
I study the last of my pint, broken white waves up the glass
                        it would be so nice if John were here
                        I allow myself to acknowledge that
then to phone

It went well, thank god. No one
booed me, some good questions
afterwards. All great stuff for the book
I think. How are you getting on?

                    You star.
                    Always knew you'd smash it.

                    I send a photo of my hand
                    by the almost-empty glass
                    wooden table ring-marked

He replies immediately.
The George?

                    Bingo. 50 points to you.

Who you with?

                    Just me
                    And my pint.

Good idea. You deserve a pint.

                    *Pints

Those too.

                    Well done babe. Must feel great
                    to have done it. Steinheads not
                    driving you mad yet?

Not yet . . .

                    Assimilation, complete.

Dinner soon, still time for a spat
before the night is over

You been looking after yourself?

                    Yeah taking it easy over here

Sounds like it if you're in The George
No better place

hovering over my phone
thumbs twitching
over what I could type
but I don't
I don't tell John about Julia
or how alive death seems
none of that needs to exist

as if he hears my pause
Love you Ro
Call me whenever.

Texting your husband?   back to it
Boyfriend, yes.
Is he coming to save you from the strange man?
Not quite yet. He said to humour you for a bit.
He puts down our pints and clinks our last two together,
returning them to the bar. I realise that I have no idea who this
man is, haven't even registered what he looks like.
Not properly. Not enough to hold on to.

Blue eyes? (maybe)
Fifties?   (maybe)

How old are you? I ask, when he's back,
interested in startling him.
Twenty-one or so.
Or so?

Plus twenty years.
Plus twenty years or so?
Perhaps.

    I'm improvising,
    not sure really what I'm saying or what I want from this
    though   yes,
    I like how I can escape into someone else's concerns

I watch in the pause as his gaze moves idly to my mouth
bottom lip reacts   pushing forward just a little
could be innocent   is innocent   only here for a pint
though   (I allow myself the thought)
                         (there to push away)
I could fuck him   (yet)
that twitch of interest anyone there to discover
it's not a feeling I need any more
particularly not with a man who usually I would ignore
I could know all of him
                this, it's not want
                only possibility

to live out a life I have no interest in living
but then a missile of spit lands on my cheek as he says
Do you live round here?
and the track evaporates
                It's not that I'm repulsed
                but I'm in my head,
                one step back from him.

Can I tell you something?   remembering
drunk   tipsy more honest   on the brink
        Alice's mum laughing,
            cigarette wedded to the ledge between two fingers
This was real,   I know I thought that.
Jesus, this is real.

Come out here, Alice had said.   Mischievous.
Through the door then handing me a cigarette   and a grin
coughing smoke, throat hit, her face
clouding   not so much a fall as a loss

Cigarette that bad?   I said

Can I tell you something?

I should've said yes but I was a kid
So I said,   No
crossing my arms for emphasis
as if there was no chance I'd listen

Rosa!
I'm joking!
Well now I don't want to say.

Red-tipped cigarette, face dark

I know this memory immediately
not one of those I need to pinpoint

scrabble in the soil to find the roots
no no, this one is easy to pull up

You know you're my best mate, Alice, don't you?
Yeah, and you're mine. For ever and ever amen.

So tell me!

Yesterday, she said.
A man tried to follow me home.
Just for a bit.

                    In the dark, neither of us had a face.
                             Only a suggestion.

What happened? I asked, and she emitted a sound

     E u r r r r r r g h h h h .

Then it was a foreign sound. Guttural, earthy,
but I know it now.
The frustration of having to word something that should
never have happened. It's trudging, heavy work.

Eurrrrrrghhhh, she said, and I took her hand.
Gentle. Struck by how tiny it felt. A kid's hand.
     I don't know what the surprise was. We were kids.
He walked beside me for a bit. Said he had something he
thought I might like to see. Was like a fucking PSHE video.
Then he started unzipping his jeans and I just ran.

Did he keep following?
No clue. Hope not. Didn't look. All I could hear was the
thump of my schoolbag hitting my back. It was properly
slowing me down. I kept thinking about those highlighters
I'd been showing off in science. If it's them that slow me
down, if they let him catch me up, then it's punishment,
you know what Mrs Clark loves to say: Pride before a fall.

Shut up that is not how it works,
but I'm glad you're okay, what a creep.
                    I tried to put my arms around her
                    but she was stiff   in the remembering

Alice was the first person I wanted to tell when I was raped.
Too late. Nineteen. Yet still sure if she had been there I could
have emitted that too-early-for-words sound
and she would have waited   knowing I had something to say
but knowing too   it was work.

By the time I met John it was far off   over-rehearsed
hard to remember its rawness

the frustration in my throat   not wanting to have to say it
                              can that be true?
I don't know whether it was that I had moved on from it
or whether I had faced myself away

so sure of how these scraps are sewn up
                              relegated to the past

                                        but can that be true?
Had always thought of life as a chronological line
not convinced of that now, not in this moment, no, too simple
it's more enmeshed, should be something denser
easier to be submerged in
easier to lose your place.

Mouthful of beer
followed by another
pub warmed by company   anonymous
two women squealing,
their hands glued to each other's shoulders
men in a circle as if they're concealing something

and this man here, clearing his throat in a wet cough
I left my wife last year, he tells me. *We had been together since
school,* he tells me. *And I woke up one morning and thought
FUCK, I was bored, to be honest, so bored I hadn't the energy
to realise I was bored. I don't know. Maybe the boredom only
arrived on that day, but I suddenly didn't want anything that I
had in my life.*

It sounds like you're describing a midlife crisis, I tell him,
caught between cautious and mean.
No. It was genuine. I wanted rid of everything.
*Is that possible? To erase it all? If someone has been part of your
life for ever, kicking them out doesn't get rid of them even if you
never see them again.*
You can try.

Oh, I know you can try. I'm just not so sure it works.
You're thinking about yourself, I'm thinking about me. Maybe
women are worse at letting go.
It worked then?
Yep, he says,
lips protruding as he eases a mouthful from the glass.
And what did you decide to do with your life instead?
I hear it in my voice, a harshness. I don't even know this man
but part of me wants to break him. I don't point out that he
is in a pub on his own on a Friday night.
To be fair, so am I.
I can tell you one thing I'm not fucking doing.
What?
Eating fucking mince for Friday dinner at 7 p.m. on the dot.

Tonight   he fills the space
takes my brother's place; stands on his stage.
In short, he's welcome.

What do you do then?
Oh, a bit of journalism, a bit of teaching.
English degree then?
He's got me there
Yes, that's me. A predictable graduate for you.
        Never thought I'd be telling someone that:
        a bit of teaching
        once I was done at school, that would be it, I was sure
        no chance of going back

Would never have arrived here on my own.
It was John, after all,
as I fretted about the risks of freelancing full-time
who had said,

        That academy school Mike used to work for,
         they're starting a literacy initiative.
So?
        They're looking for readers to work with kids . . .

I would never have thought,
if John hadn't been the one to broach
but him asking allowed me   to   well   made it obvious
of course, that is what I should do
blind until told   of course it would suit me, move me
to observe how things can be   to help

        even if I do still scan for patterns   always

even Margo   listening out for hints about her brother
        always that jittery caution
what should be harmless   somehow   kaleidoscopic
    shifting between
no proof, no reason why she, why they, should be anything
like me, like us
        all of it distant, how much of it really me
        scared me, hesitant me, sometimes yes
        but none of that is me now, not really

What about you? I ask him. *What do you do?*

Oh, I've done all sorts. Laying lines, tunnelling, over the last
couple of years I've done more carpentry, I was fed up with the
hours, but I think that's where it all went wrong, being around,
suddenly having the time to question

he stares at his hands by his pint   thick, roughened skin
                                          could stroke that palm
                                          check for softness
                    What did it make you realise?

he looks up   can't read his expression
He considers saying . . .
    Your generation love to talk about their feelings, don't they?
I suspect that anyway   in the pause as he tilts his pint.
Just enough to introduce a swell of tide
                                before straightening the glass.
            . . . I don't fucking know, he says.
            That I'm too old? That it's all a bit late?
He halts. I don't say anything. Keeping my face open.
Letting him throat-clear with his initial sentences. Warm-up
gargling. Something is coming. I know that much.

Tom, my son, has never been very well. I worked a lot for the
money for him   that was what I always said it was
money for treatment   for the just-in-cases as well as the
inevitables   but god was it easy not to be around
that's what I realised, too late. I don't think I did it all . . . right.

I'm sorry. There's never a right way to react

to something like that.
No, there is. You be there, you talk, you
listen. And that's not what I did.

On the way home I get voicemail but talk anyway
I'm walking back from the pub now, had a few drinks, and I miss
you, I tell John's phone and mine, neither of which are listening.
Mum keeps calling but I can't answer, I don't know why, I don't
know why I can't. Haven't heard her voice since, I know it's
weird, bad of me really, we've texted but I can't, I, she'll be upset
and I'll have to comfort her. I can't deal with that now, don't
want to have to be that. Agh. I'm drunk aren't I. I was talking
to a man in the pub who doesn't like mince. I think he wanted to
fuck me but that could be a misreading, what do I know. I wish
you were here to hug me to sleep, I wish I could go back a week
and stay there ignorant for ever. Any chance of making that
happen? Keep me updated. I should probably stop talking to
your phone. I have a feeling it's not going to talk back.
Not today.
Phone lights up, white by my ear. Mum.
Unbelievable. Mum's calling. Maybe she's been listening. If you
were here you'd say JUST ANSWER IT, but you're not so I
won't. Sorry.

How do you deal with an unwanted guest?
There are many answers   infinite once you get particular.
Perhaps I should refine the question:

How do I deal with the lingering traces of my brother
a brother I never fully understood
a brother who will not leave me the fuck alone?

Women are good   or bad
with unwanted guests   depending on the metric
they are good
no, stop
I am good   at accommodating
my brother would say   Hey, sis!
and at the very least I would look up
                         acknowledge

start soft
assume the best

I cannot push   I learnt long ago
that I did not have the power to push
resist   to wiggle out   for all my life I have been pinned
so yes   I nod, move, shift, allow
                      is it allowing if there is no other possibility?

Can't start to regret
it would be a shame   a great shame
if his death made me want to stage a reunion

no chance, no chance
but he has   pressed a switch

opened a gate
does he remember

              would he remember
did he

              breaking the lock on the bathroom door?

I desperately pulled my dress on once I realised it wasn't going
to hold shut   and I never knew

did he?

            was he trying to see me?

Dad at work
     vulnerable
in not knowing whether I was
not knowing whether I needed to protect

it would have made sense
suppressed fury
discomfort at what he felt
not able to bear me   as a woman

        oh, I have theorised this before,
        chewed over this one already,
        give it a break, give all of it a break
        I know it can't be right, not completely

It didn't start when my body arrived

he had already hurt me

used to pinch his fingers around my ankles
gripping either side of the tendon at the back
he worked out it hurt
and stuck with it

I'd be in bed, Dad having said goodnight
then   Night little sis
settling by the bed
his hands pincering
trying to kick free
but him pinching still

the next morning I would arch my feet
and send lightning up my calves

no, it had already started.

Saturday

I never witnessed the whispered screams
voices pitching high before being dialled down to a hiss

                                or at least, I don't carry them with me
Mum seemed distracted and unbothered
and I didn't mind

it wasn't that I began to miss Mum
although of course I did
of course I would rather life had continued on as it was,
Dad happy, Mum drifting between,
there to stroke my hair
or laugh too loudly at the TV
but no   it wasn't just that
I had lost another presence, another witness.

If he was wound up, on the brink of what was then unfamiliar
she would dance with him   (or if he was unwilling
                                swing him onto her shoulders)
and Mum would sing,

                What do you do with a drunken sailor
            what do you do with a drunken sailor
                        what do you do with a drunken sailor
                early in the morning

too much whisky in this boy's cereal,
she would crow
shaking her head.

Sometimes, she would walk him in curved lines
Look at him! can't even walk the plank straight!
and in between she would sing
      drunken sailor
my drunken sailor   only getting louder if he cried or shouted
so that her voice reached the edges, wrapping round his like
a wet towel stifling a fire

I considered Mum when, as a teenager, I psychologised
posing myself questions
for example:

               Why is your brother a nightmare?

               (and)

               Does he even want to be better?

               (and)

               Are you sure you're related?

other questions too
all circulating around the same idea
which really
more than anything
was an exclamation   fuck!
or worse
a gesture

at its centre, yes, just simply
head banging against the wall, enough, enough, enough

Mum was the only one who seemed to know how to react,
who could say something with the confidence that it would
lift his mood

I would think back to her tactics: him over her shoulder,
or insisting everyone turned silent so we could hear the
conversation of the neighbours next door,
                                    could we make out the words?

Once she fell to the ground and stage-whispered:

                    Save
                    Mum
                    from
                    the
                    floor

There wasn't a formula
and I worried   then learnt
that her solutions were hers
in my hands they were nothing

it was her, he had decided, who could help
that was all

before we discovered that it was Mrs Clark's son

who had killed the animals on the Skinners' farm
I suspected my brother

I would remind myself
sternly
that my brother had cried when Mum left
as if someone who cries isn't capable of murder.

I do not know where I am

for a beat

then   bed warm

knowing of my body

yes   of course   exactly where it is most likely I would be
on waking up

absent John a confusion
and

oh   (oh)

I am in bed   yes,
and   there is a vice locked against my head

jaws clamped firm

only explanation,

the only explanation is that
                         there is a vice locked against my head
not opening my eyes yet but seeing it,
                              imagining what must be there
gripping, slowly being winched   so yes seeing it

I am not in a Martin Scorsese
but why else would my head feel like this?

yes, there were pints   five, maybe,
                                               could be wrong
                      wasn't counting, didn't need to, didn't think to

even so,
I cycle through the arguments   eyes shut to the world
groaning, a little   can allow myself a little groan

hangovers should be illegal they should be put in prison
                         abolish all prisons, yes
                         but make a new one in their place
                         for hangovers

a government department for hangovers
a weekly stipend for hangover recoverers

it's my fault   this   can't argue with that
but I'm going to get myself in gear   get over it
get out of it   shower, water, food.

        Easy.

By the end of the shower   more awake
brighter   clean   yes   I'm getting over it

        this is something I can fix   (focus on)

yes   I'm getting over it.

When I check my phone   showered, stomach moving
I have a text from Mum   I delay
John first   a missed call
and
Hey love,
Tried to call you, are you alright?
You sounded lovely and tipsy in your
voicemail, but a bit sad too. All things
you're justified to feel and be but still.
I'm going to try and speak to Erika
today instead. Text me when you're up,
I love you. X

        The drama of a few pints . . .

Gunna chill out today and do fuck-all. Well done again on last night, sounds like you did great. Hope everything goes good today too. X

He's online!
Want to call?

Not now, got urgent mission of coffee and shower. Later?

Sound like good missions.
Deal. X

I pace the flat, using my legs as distraction

in the living room   a frame that was on the wall
sits content face-up on the sofa

       too many times have I woken to John close
       Rosa? Are you okay?
       tube of mascara in my hand or half-dressed

I know how to reason,
who to suspect if something is out of place
       Can we leave the washing-up for your night self?

not funny now
alone, a photo of John and me staring back
wall holding an absence, one cratered nail

my sleep self likes to startle
You're going to need to hide the knives, I joked to John,
then regretted.
It was funny until you said that.
Now a portion of my brain will be wondering,
every night, if you're going to stab me.

You and me both.

A silence. Before I grinned. Sorry, I said.
Don't be, I could overpower you with two eyes closed.
It was nice, I thought, how that didn't scare me.
Then horrible that I was pleased not to be afraid.

My alter ego has been infrequent.
I put her off with suspicion.
I thought she was offended, or considerate. But here she is.
This.

        must be her

        (cannot allow other interpretations)

        (like, for example, not that we're getting into it,
        but just to pose a theory, throw it out there,
        make a quiet insinuation, like, for example,
        what if it were your brother?)

He always had a good sense of humour, my brother
or at least, innate comic timing
never missed a beat.

I hang the frame up.
Never happened.
And I check my phone.
Ready now to open Mum's message.

Don't freak out but I'm on the train.
You haven't been answering and I
just want to see you sillyhead.
Be there by 12 x

11:30. Jesus. I consider leaving her with the affront of an
empty house, going anywhere that isn't here.
But I don't
I make coffee   and I wait.

Have you heard from him recently?
a question he had never tried before
yet attempted to land as regular.
A normal, usual line of questioning. Chit-chat really.
Dad. We don't talk. Haven't. Five years.
Time only goes in one direction but nice try.

He hesitated. Flattened his hands and moved them in a
square as if he were cleaning the shower door to see through.

I remember that. Strange new ground.
He didn't know what to say.
He was trying to reset   restart the attempt
                          without knowing the best approach
uncharted waters   all that
I gave an offering: Dad, it's not on you
it's not your fault,   not your responsibility.
Then, he still felt there was a chance.   Jesus.
One year left of my brother then.
Six years practising his death. Building his absence.

Mum was different. Less arms-reach-out. Snippier.

          It's embarrassing, Rosa. You two not talking.
          Between the two of you you're loading up
          therapists' trolleys.
          It was a divorce, not a mass murder.

Always the divorce, as if our feelings were only because of
her and Doughnut Man

(to be fair it scans)   for him, yes, at first, it scans
                not at first   that's not fair
                                              not at first
At first, we were close   brought close

Hug please.   Playing Connect 4 obsessively as distraction.
               The studious slot-click.
               He was eleven, he should've won,

but he sucked.
Tongue between his teeth,   missing opportunities
I felt adult, designated my duty.   (keep him happy)
So I let him win   again and again   checking his face
moved to witness him lost for a moment   back to nothing.

Doorbell. That recognisable cold buzz.

I don't startle. I know. Mum.
Hand on mug, I continue to sit as if uninterrupted. Almost
dizzy in the delay.
Peace where I should be moving.

                              Get up.
I instruct myself.
                              And I do.

Oh, Rosa, sweetheart. She grips me in a hug, her sleeves and
bag unfurling in the movement, instantly familiar, here she
is!, always chaos, extra layers haphazard around her like a
chicken after a face-off, feathers disordered.

I don't recognise how she smells
if my eyes were closed, she could be anyone

When your dad called I couldn't believe it
her eyes are bloody   red swirls like ink in water

I couldn't get through to you and I just wanted to see you,
make sure you were okay.
It's a shock.
Had you talked recently?
No, I say

> (discounting him on the steps
> weeks ago
> right where she is fussing
> no sorry no, door closed).

Oh, she says, *well,* she says,
I saw him last month,
he came to visit me and Brian,
unexpected, and we spoke about a lot of things
and, Rosa, he—
it was as if he knew he wouldn't be here now,
he had such a clarity: he knew what he needed to say, who he
needed to speak to, like he was ticking off some list, I don't know,
I'm looking at it strangely now, of course I am, everything is
strange in death, but I hadn't seen him in two years—

You hadn't seen him in two years?
I knew it was infrequent but   I can't remember
I didn't realise it had got worse.   whether I knew already

He went quiet on me. Didn't explain why. Only responded after
I left him messages saying I wanted to know if he was alive and
okay. I told you at the time because I wanted to check if he was in
contact with you.

I don't remember Mum asking. But the answer would have been simple: no.

But anyway, having ignored me for so long, suddenly he comes to see me. Last month. And he said he was going to speak to you, Rosa, he seemed sure of that, he must have meant to.

What could he have to say to me?

Hadn't seen it that way before. How him coming to the door was a thread drawing back of intention. Of speaking about doing it. Of thinking about what to say. Of planning it. I hadn't considered that he might have had some theoretical script in his head, inevitably strayed from once it turned real, but going over and over it nonetheless.

What did he want to say to me?

I don't know, he seemed so reflective, so sure of what he needed to do, it was silly, I told him then, I know he was an angry boy—
An angry boy? He was a bit more than an angry boy.

We are on my doorstep, still, just where he was a month ago, still
we both stand   waiting
but I cannot bring myself to invite her in

Instead, I say,

He was probably trying to make amends,
now he was living with someone.

Yes,   she says,   *that might be it.*

So you knew?

He told me when he visited   about Julia   yes
He wanted to, he, I really thought you would have seen him.

He turned up here   *last month*
                        her face waits   expectant
I closed the door on him.
                        Oh Ro—
I don't regret it! I won't, I can't, Mum, you don't know what he
fucking did and you don't seem to care or want to know or
    I have to stop I have to stop he's dead and Mum won't I can't
it's a lot to process
he wasn't exactly uncomplicated.

She laughs, a high-pitched fluctuation like a creaking swing

Yes he had his complications

can I?   she gestures to the door.

                    That's why Mum and Dad had kids
                    I once told my brother

(as a joke, but eventually I believed it too)
because they had run out of things to say
kids are a talking point, after all,
more problems than delight,
but always something.

What happened here? Mum asks
     only then do I see the kitchen as someone else
   cupboards open   mugs undrunk
a plate   when did that break?   in pieces on the floor.
She leans down and brushes ceramic splinters with the edge
of her hand, her coat catching the ground
         collecting the shards in her palm
Oh,   *I think I knocked it*   *thanks.*
She tilts her hand to me in a question   I point to the bin
then she sits   easily
I stand   not knowing how to let my arms be
cupping an elbow

Mum looks at her hands, the table, her feet
Have you been doing okay?   I ask, fetching her gaze
she shakes her head as if to replace sound
(to show: what could I say in place of this?
        impossible to fit the words in)
I hadn't even thought to prepare, she says,
realising she should speak, *I hadn't even . . . thirty,*
what a horrible, young, neat age.

Thirty? Can that be right?
There's something adult about it.
Not that he wasn't before. Not that I'm not.
But it feels distant   for him to be thirty
is for him not to be him at all
3rd February   what was I doing on his birthday?
Often I clock the date, but I'm not sure I even did this year
passing without me realising it had passed

I remembered on the way here, she says,
about the biscuit contest.
What was that?
Oh it was classic. A bored Saturday after we had got the shop in.
I suggested you both see how many biscuits you could fit into your
mouth. You complained because your mouth was smaller   always
the pedant   I insisted no, those were the rules
but when he went to fetch the biscuits, he put a pack of custard
creams in front of you and gave himself the digestives.
She sees my lack of reaction
          speaks like she's pulling my chosen card from the pack
He gave you the smaller biscuits. Slipped them in front of you like
it wasn't a gesture.

Sounds like a Nobel Peace Prize–winning incident.
How did we do?

I can't really remember. There was a lot of mess,
and a lot less time taken up than I had hoped.

That's not the biscuits story I remember
we had a deal   unspoken
if we nicked a biscuit from the tin,
                    we'd take two
finding the other and placing it in their hand,
or on the sofa arm, before disappearing
to crunch our own

          one night I was out, seeing Alice
          and I came home to a Hobnob
          on my bedroom carpet,
          pushed through the gap
          between the door and the floor

Mum would want to hear that,
easy to imagine how she'd soften
but I don't want to give it up
as if it disproves me   harsher with her
                    harshness all through me
                    when did it become like this?

Have you met Julia?   I ask
                    pushing things on   needing to.
No, no, just spoken to her on the phone. But we all will at the
funeral. I wish he'd been able to introduce us himself,
I guess he didn't know there was a rush
                    she drums her fingers on the table
finger   by finger   by finger
dull din   fills my head

        a tap a poke a nudge as she keeps on
        insisting against the table, one-tone jab
so quick for anything to grate, with Mum
too quick, really   for it to be anything to do with her
        all me, surely

Do you remember the kid,   I ask, still standing against the side
studying the kitchen cabinet before
                gliding   like moving down a scale
                note to note,
                        to meet her eyes
who killed those animals on the Skinners' farm?

                        She tilts her head, softly curious.
I thought it was arson? she says, reaching a higher note.
What?
That Clark kid, she says, *what was his name . . . Toby? Didn't he
set alight one of their barns?*
*No, well maybe, but he killed half the animals. I stopped working
there afterwards, he was arrested, I don't know what happened
to him in the end.*
I remember the arrest, she frowns in recollection, *your dad told
me on the phone, but I'm sure I would've remembered
something like that . . . We were worried, I remember that much,
with you working there,
whether you were safe, or*   one-burst laugh
if you'd get any ideas.

        I wanted to tell her now, as a way of explaining,

who I had suspected   but smaller suddenly
in her laugh, it becomes a different memory
diminished, somehow

I'm not making it up.
I'm sure you're not . . . you know how differently kids take
things in.
I was fourteen, not six.
Fourteen,   she says, like it's a precious jewel   *fourteen.*
I shouldn't have asked. You weren't there,
why would you remember the details?
She purses her mouth, drawing it in small, here she goes,
that mouth means, here she bloody goes, my daughter on the
attack, ready to berate me for having a life, for daring to be
happy, for choosing what I wanted, here she bloody goes . . .

                         she taps, again, nail on wood
Can you not?
What?   still tapping   a line Dad would say comes to me
                         You'll bloody drill a hole through that.

I go with
You're tapping.
Oh   she puts her hands in her lap
                    cradled there,
                    as if they've personally been offended.

I had wanted to delay. Instead.
One word at a time. That's all it is. Time to say.

Mum?

I know how this will go.
I watch as it happens.

She knows too in the way she looks up and doesn't say Yes?,
or What, love? She holds back, giving nothing that could
help draw a sentence from me
I know you weren't around as much, not that that releases you,
but you didn't see what he was like with me. You knew someone
else. You didn't know who he was to me. There was just. I spent
so much time growing up absolutely fucking terrified. I don't
think you get how much time I spent full of fear and anxiety of
what might happen next, in the very place I should have felt
protected
motionless presence   stirs me on
defending before she speaks
                              knowing already she doesn't believe me
this isn't a case of some arguments, or him winding me up when I
would rather have been left alone, that's not what it was.

Still, she says nothing
sitting at the kitchen table with her bag and coat wound
around her

Mum, he used to hurt me.   *Sweetheart, you were kids.*
                              quick out of her mouth, a reflex.
Teenagers,
and he was older, stronger, and he hurt me.

186

What? he punched you? slapped you? what did he do?
He did everything! He intimidated me. Hurt me. Threw me to
the floor. Would keep his nails long so he could easily cut my skin
and then just poke poke poke. I got a fucking infection on my
back from it
why, why, why does it sound like nothing, how can I make it
sound like something
remember the collarbone?
Sweetheart   sweetheart
                    she fumbles for words I do not want to hear
he died   that brings up a lot of emotions
it will mess with your head a bit
I'm not saying that he didn't but—

You know what he did to Alice don't you?
Kids, my love
that was tragic, but that wasn't him.
We never spoke about Alice
none of us
not Mum, not Dad, not my fucking brother

it was a tragedy,
that was agreed   shutters down, no more to be said
a tragedy   hugs, pats, shaking head

my brother refused to discuss her
months after, I would continue to conduct conversations
imagining what he wouldn't say
not hurt but sly

taunting myself   half becoming him

                              The thing about Alice,
I would perform, ventriloquising my brother
                        was that she did
                        exactly what I asked her to.

I didn't want to hear it
but my head would torment   not my own

keeping going, even now
                       I used to humiliate her
his voice understated
luxuriating
in your head you can echo anyone and hear their resonances.
                       I would tell her she was disgusting
                       she would look beautiful, jesus christ,
                       and I would turn to her, as if to say
                       Wow, look at you
                       then I'd twist, turn my face acid
                       and say, You look horrible.
                       You look fucking hideous.

                       I'd text her at school
                       knowing she was in Mrs Gordon's lesson
                       and say   Go to the toilets now
                       and take a photo of your tits
                       And she would! It was amazing, really
                       anything I wanted or didn't want

but insisted on anyway
all of it, she would give me

He shared those photos of her
I'm sure
how else could it have happened

there was no one at school who didn't see
I didn't, though
I didn't
I never looked
hints on people's phones, maybe
I'd move away but would have already been confronted
flesh on screen is savage   stands out

but I never looked

once those photos were released
skin too young
people would laugh at Alice
it was something they had imagined
described in detail
teased at, wanked over, but seeing it?
humiliating
she was disgusting

                                        Then she needed him,
                                        even more

My brother was worse after Alice died
I realised how much had been held back
split between us

it wasn't just a renewed energy
it was as if he had refined how to be brutal

before, it was clumsy
after, it was expert
once he had latched on to a move: pinching, twisting my wrists
he would practise it, over and over, until it became a skill
he let his thumbnails lengthen
jabbing them into the small of my back until they cut
I'd twist round in the mirror and see half-moons.

I know it must be hard for you   turning him away
not seeing him before he died
but don't make it worse for yourself, sweetheart,
just take it slowly.

Looking at her   I see everything
In her is it all, again and again, time-loop repetition, and
now being the last one, the only one left who acknowledges
what he could be, who will admit that it is there,
feel it boiling, under me, in me   can't keep it in
What would I have to say? What would I have to say?
I am standing here, right in front of you, and it's like he's pulling
at your arm, talking into your ear.

Why am I always nothing? It's like I'm not even speaking.

Nothing to show.

I had the same conversation with Dad
younger then, more hopeful of an end
                    It can't be that bad, he had said.
                    You know what you two are like
                    you wind each other up.

That's not what this is
that's not it at all

but there was nothing I could say
insisting would be evidence of childishness; backing down
evidence of lying

Please, Dad
I said,
softly
this is serious.

He looked at me fully then, not preparing to look elsewhere
I could see I had his attention and the surprise of it hurt

he looked pained too
we did not make it easy, we were not simple
now I was telling him
Dad

I cannot bear it
I cannot bear it, Dad
as if there was any choice
I could not change my brother
my dad could not change my brother
my brother could not change my brother

seeing me provoked him   that was what I knew
stay out of his way   that was what I knew

he did not like being reminded of me at school
particularly not when one of his mates would nod his head
and say   Alright   it's your little sis,
                          grabbing his elbow to slow him down.
                          Not so little really, is she,
                          look at her, all grown up.

                          think of his mate   Dylan
                          hadn't I
                          done exactly what he feared
                          pre-empted

Those conversations were dangerous
not because my brother would say anything
but because he didn't

he would redden
pulling at the corners of his trouser pockets

containing

                        overactive imagination
all of this
                                        an exaggeration

no
                        I lived it
it was true

            hadn't always been nothing   no
            with Dylan, he had twigged
            someone telling him
            still I fear don't I   that it was Dylan
                        showing off   miming touching me
                        or how I went down on him
                        seeing his hand, in a crowd of boys,
                        mimicking how he pushed
                        at the back of my head

that didn't happen though, it didn't you never saw him do that
you never knew   never confirmed   that he had told anyone
but hadn't it happened, the Monday after we had got together
                                    home from school
yes   home from school and my brother there already

                You've been texting him.

reaching for me
to wrestle my phone   and running to the toilet in a panic
how to cover?   no time to delete all the messages
                         part of me not wanting to either
until tapping
         fucking genius, I am   I must have said that to myself
         screaming   CAN'T I EVEN PEE IN PEACE?
         as I changed Dylan's name in my phone to 'Alice'

flushing with heart beating   would this work
walking back out without knowing
                                 what was going to happen next
yet   scrolling through my texts with his forehead furious
it had   mining deeper yet nearly all just Alice Alice Alice

what does any of this add up to?

it was Dylan   wasn't it   not me   who had said
This is fun   but none of it is worth the hassle
                your brother is nuts when you're involved.

He chose to be friends with him, surely that's   something
                                 a speck of proof
                                 but what it proves,
                                 I don't know.

Mum, I can't do this right now
I feel bad saying not now, you got the train, but I didn't ask you

and I need some lunch and some space, it's horrible, a tragedy
but we all need different things right now.
Is John here?
No, he's at a conference.
She looks at me with startled eyes
I said he should go!
we can't all stop for this.

Oh it's horrible it's horrible it's horrible it's horrible.

She is speaking more to herself than me
her whole body sinks, wilts, drawing into herself

hate seeing her upset   me making her that way
                        or at least, making it even worse
but I'm scared of what else I will say
and while she sits here saying
Horrible horrible horrible horrible.
                        I see my brother
                        corner of my eye

                        he moves like a shark,
                        there then gone.

Something in the way she says horrible
there is something in the way she says horrible
that I cannot hear
she says   horrible   and I hear a truth

in her voice   *horrible*
is my brother   *horrible*   gone
is my brother   *horrible*   dead

I cannot.   Am not.

          Unsteadied by her.

And I see my brother.

                      Ghost trace.

                      Raised by it.
                      Encouraged.

No,   I can't   I have to push
can only push.

Sorry, Mum,   I say.
It takes all my effort to get her out
to find the words.
Let's talk soon, okay.   too formal, stiff, but all I can manage

Her exit is mechanic
head moving towards me then doorway then back
arms glitching   not knowing whether to hug
what direction to go in   rigid exercise
then gone.

Depression is a type of intelligence
that's what someone said, after Alice died

Depression is a type of intelligence, they said,
Alice able to see beyond the systems
a revelation which was impossible to return from

it was bullshit
but I found it reassuring
that she had taken her life because she was too smart

Alice, they said, was unable to contain what we had been
taught to contain, meant to only acknowledge frames one at
a time, so we can keep on going

she was depressed
it wasn't a clarity
but it was nice to consider
to designate any meaning, even if it couldn't last

she was special, Alice
but isn't that simply what death brands someone you loved?

After Alice died
I became sure I was depressed
as if it were infectious
I was miserable
but I feared that I too would kill myself,
that I couldn't contain it either

stuck in a bird's-eye view, impossible to reset

I was sixteen   maybe it was selfish   but what did I know?

I started a self-assessment online
and stopped on the third question

HAVE YOU FOUND YOURSELF
FEELING DEPRESSED?
if I knew what feeling depressed felt like
I wouldn't be doing an online assessment
to see if what I was feeling was depression

if I could realise this,   I reasoned
if I could mock an online form
that was the proof I needed that I was okay

(maybe it was effective after all)

being a teenager is the most emotional,
and most shallow, experience without comparison
not recognising one day that a feeling will be done

feeling advances   works towards completion
you have to learn that.

As soon as Mum is down the stairs from the kitchen,
front door tentatively closed,

mouth unsaying,
I fetch my coat.
John on my phone.
No dice with Erika,
she's being prickly . . .

> quickly fielding
> **You can talk tomorrow,**
> **it's soon enough!** 😊

Fresh air.   That's the thing.   Fresh air.

> You could have told her about the bacon
> laid on your pillow in the middle of the night
> inches from your mouth

> but what would be the point
> people react differently

> if I told Sarah she would say
> What the fuck what the fuck what the fuck
> categorically, one hundred per cent messed up
> But Mum? I can predict how it would go
> You know what kids are like, my love
> we all do silly things

if I told Sarah
feels distant   saw her, when, yesterday?
the idea of teaching, school
goldfish like cod-liver
all of that   different path.

In the park, I rest   just for a moment   peace
tuning in to anything that isn't my own head   peace

You can avoid all those conflicts,   a woman behind
                                   my shoulder says
though I don't turn around.

You can push them down or you can push towards them,
it's a choice.
I keep sitting on the bench. Staring at a man in the shadow
of a tree. He moves his hand, holding a cigarette, rigid
yet flamboyant
as if he is being filmed (early take)

      There is something about me that makes men mad
      the conviction comes to me from I don't know where
                            I don't know why
      but I know it to be true
      there is something about me that makes men mad
      I give off something they want to get rid of
      fists pounding down

      sick,   like a dying bird
      best to twist her neck   see her out now,   quick.

Find a phrase, find something that deflects or protects you.
I did,   the woman listening tells her,   *I fucking did.*
But after the first night, it stopped working.
It was like a temporary magic charm. Worked for one use,

then nothing, trying it again but fucking nothing.
So I started walking. I told myself just for a while. Just a stretch.
But I kept on. Three hours later I was still walking, couldn't turn
back.

A baby hangs from a dad's front, red cheeks, breath.
Look at those legs.   I almost say it   Legs!
in constant fall from the sling   slinky, boneless tentacles

What did they say, she asks, *when you got back?*
Nothing. Nothing out of the ordinary anyway. I don't think they
noticed I had gone.

Stand up. Try this walking thing.

Don't look behind   don't sneak a look
don't grab a detail   don't compare with my imagination
patchwork scarf, mole on her lip
                              don't allow myself any of it
Voices, that is all I let them be. Voices.

Where would I get to if I walked for three hours?
                              Nowhere.
                              You'd walk in circles.
                              Fall down as soon as three was up.
                              Down on the ground in the exact spot
                              dizzy as fuck.

It was Freshers' Week   easy to remember   to date it

when he texted, said he'd be in London

                              half-insisted we meet
                              (by not presenting options)

I wouldn't be able to say where now, then I didn't know any
streets, can't recognise from my memory

grey day is all I know
dense, impenetrable sky, cloud barriers

We'd met because he had said,   Here, 11 a.m.,
                              I'm in London, come.
And I had.
I don't know what I went to him expecting.

Keeping to his pace
I waited   even for an acknowledgement
leaving him gaps

until I had to fill them.

Is your plan to just pretend none of it happened?

None of what?

Come on. Don't try that.

Rosa, I'm trying to be an adult here. I know we haven't always got on, but you're my sister, you're at uni, I thought you might be ready.

You've cut your nails, I said.

Pause.
He must have kept walking but that's not how I see it.
Everything halted. On pavement, still. Looking forward.
Paused.
He looked at his hands, confused for a second, maybe, I'll give him that, then deciphering

                    tucking fingers in   nails hidden in fists
Shut up, he said. Shut up shut up shut up.

                Walking, now I know we were walking.

You're impossible, Rosa.

What was the point, he said to himself, speaking the same thought in different ways as he spun, about-turn, then down the stairs to the Tube

unsaid   clear   Don't follow.

So I didn't.
First year of uni; I was someone else then.
Of course I was.

So much since   could only guess at

I know what to do   cold of outside like a newsflash.
Encouraging myself home, following the path I know,
moving quickly, almost running, the frustration of wanting
to be home yet having to get there,
fast-stepping
                    until
door unlocked,   up the stairs,   lights on as I go
I move my arms back to wiggle coat off me
kicking feet out of shoes at the same time
plant myself onto bed   comfort of duvet underneath

I've already drafted the text on my hurry back
words warm in head   but stiff to type

**Hey Dad, I thought I might try and
talk to Julia before the funeral,
she must be struggling.
Could I have her number?**

Done.

Dad gets back in minutes.
His speed pulls at my chest   he is alone,
                    must be desperate for anything.

I see him in a doorway, leaning towards his phone, an off-

balance, strange attention focused in on something so small,
like holding a baby
I realise   imagining him   and my heart! at the thought
that I am writing over   this is a memory

standing in the kitchen doorway so long that I had to look
up and pretend to sigh   What is it, Dad?

Expecting nothing, or something, but not what he said,
which was: It's funny, which was: You know I miss your
Mum, we all do, but I've got better at refining what it is that
I miss.
She's not dead, Dad, I interjected.
Yes, no, sorry, but I did lose her, sweetheart,
in a great many ways I lost her.

          I had worried about my brother,
          what her absence did to him
          how no one else could soothe him like her
          and what the effect of her absence on him
          would in turn mean for me
          but I hadn't thought about Dad   not really
I should have   it should have been the first thought
it should have been obvious
unavoidable
but I hadn't
I had assumed that he was okay only because he hadn't told
me otherwise.

He had carried on standing there and I had carried on sitting
until I wondered whether that would always be us now
sitting standing   neither of us able to break
so I willed myself   until all I managed was: Dad?
Saying his name hoping it would snap him, draw him out
Dad   Dad   Dad   Dad, he only repeated
like it was an insult
still saying it to himself as he turned and left the room.

I text Julia   something my brother did once for the first time
feebly finding my voice
then I put my phone down
and I wait.
          I don't know how they met,
          don't know how he would have got her number.
          Not begging off me is all I know.

          Give me her number. Give me her number.
          Not off bloody me.

Months after I had been unprepared, when John had asked
about my brother too early, months after, we were at his
house-share.
You could reach the roof from the bathroom skylight, and
we sat on his coat, broadened into a blanket, taking turns to
inhale a joint while the other spoke.
It was a modest exchange, not quite a conversation
a gentle alternation, until

So when,   he asked, as I sucked in heat
am I going to hear about your brother?

I feel safe,   I told him
knowing you are here and he is not.

It's an old-fashioned ambition, he said next,
but you know I'm here to protect you?

I sat with that as we stayed on the roof
calm, mostly unspeaking, sometimes hand in his,
sky clear, moon a perfect cut-out, both together and apart

it was as if he stood outside time
able to push against the rest of my life
not just protecting me from future iterations of my brother
but from all of him, from even the memory

he could reverse the burden   somehow
like standing in front of the sun   blocking out.

An hour, five minutes, seconds after
he asked,   Do you think you'll see him again?
I don't know, I said. Not on purpose.

I didn't believe I ever would. I didn't think that years later
I'd be closing the door, our door, on him. I didn't think I'd
close our door and that evening John would get back from

work and I wouldn't tell him. I didn't know that three weeks later my brother would be dead. It hadn't happened, that was what I thought as I closed the door. This didn't happen. It can't. No, sorry, no.

Different though, death.

Death is a death is a death   but it was my brother.

Could roll one now
weed in the drawer, easy enough

hardly seems what I need

                                        what would I advise myself?

lying on the bed, stretching my legs until they click
hands under head

Well Dr Rosa, what do you prescribe to your patient?
Symptoms please.   My head is fucked. My brother is dead.
A dead brother is not a symptom.
                        Sorry.
Go again.
                        My head is fucked. I'm fucked.
                        I'm lonely, maybe,
                        but also resistant to company.
                        I'm restless. Tired.
                        Suffering from an acute lack of anything.

That sounds more like a diagnosis.
You're nicking my job.
                    Sorry Doc.

Didn't mention the symptom of talking to my fucking self
when really I'm waiting to see if
                    here we go: Julia.
So nice to hear from you Rosa. Skip the niceness.
It's hard to know what to say.   The passing back of sorrow.
But I'd love to see you, yes.   Scrolling to the answer I need.
I'm around tomorrow any time.
Do you have our address?

I tell myself, tomorrow. This is happening, tomorrow.

I imagine John walking through the door
the way I know I would warm, wanting to be undone
sometimes I place a hand on his shoulder   brush his cheek
and see if I can sense a reaction
                         don't know what I'm looking for
not sure what his body could reveal
yet I check
before, I was too often harsh   brittle   but with John I can't

I pool
        liquid
wax in a candle left to burn
if you nudge me, I might spill

I don't   never much
but that warming, being liquid, close to spilling
is more than I have ever been before.

Tomorrow.
Don't think of him, of now.
Of Mum sitting on the train, crying for what has passed and
what still continues. Doughnut Man at home, ready to shake
his head, a vision of support.

Don't think of that.   Bedroom disarray.
                    Think of that.
Home from seeing Alice and walking upstairs on autopilot
only to meet chaos. The absurdity of my brother's boxers,
a tin of kidney beans. The mountain of books on the bed,
pages shoving each other, splayed and intertwined, hinted
that the duvet was an afterthought,
someone realising their mistake   missed trick!
and pulling it out from underneath the pile
like a bullfighter's cape
in order to sentry it by the door.

Couldn't take it in, not at first. Was I somehow the one who
had done this? Crumpled pages. The hook of an earring
burrowing into the carpet by my foot. Senselessness, that
was the feeling.

Mum? I said   quietly   it was only my bedroom
                          only my bedroom turned to mess

but I was aware of my diary under the pillow
too late to check whether it was still there
all at once here she was, my brother just behind,
face suspiciously smoothed of all expression.

Rosa! she said.   Oh, Rosa, what are you like!
I just got back, it wasn't me,   why would I even do this?
Rosa you must stop stealing things, collecting things,
cramming things into this room, what are you even going to
do with your brother's boxers, this isn't natural. You're going
to have to put a stop to this. I'm going to have to put a stop
to this. There's only one thing for it.
                Mum's words were too rehearsed to be real,
                my brother still smooth,
                Mum the opposite (caricature concern)
So this is funny is it? I said. What was even the goal here?
You'd get me to confess to something I hadn't done? Send
me mad?

(Sheepish.) Well it's not funny when you say it like that.
You're sucking the fun out.
Brother turned round and gone.

It was a joke, love. Less amusing once you've got me spelling
out the punchline.

                my diary was missing
                    Is that right?

I remember that   but Mum was gone by the time I was
writing diaries, how could she be at home when she didn't
live there any more
                          but it happened
brother quoting the diary   you have a hard life don't you, sis
          didn't realise you hated being called fatso so much
time-collapsing riddle
                          but I remember it

I'm seeing a lot of your hand,   John says,
but not a lot of you   the comfort of his voice
are you doing okay?   and the pillow twinned,
                                     hard to tell which gives what

I'm okay   I almost believe it   closing my eyes
pretty sad   keeping in present
but I guess that's inevitable.

It's impossible to distil a state into a few handy sentences
I have no way of communicating over a phone how I am doing
so the only hope
is that my performance is convincing

over the phone all I hear is   distance
                  all I manage is   distance

John's voice in my ear is like an apparition
                                     that is close, at least

I'll be back before you know it. I could come back right now if you wanted? I know I keep offering, but it's only because I mean it.

I know you do but I'm fine thanks, love. So your talk went down well?

Yeah it did, Warthog even complimented me, can you believe it?

No he did not. What did he say?

He came up to me afterwards, and said . . . 'There's a point in that.'

Insane. He's basically nominating you for a prize.

He did pause afterwards as if I might want to kiss his hand in thanks or something.

Proud of you, love, that's so good. You're a superstar.

The OAPs have been out in force. Mel tried to sit at their table last night, mainly because we challenged her to, but they wouldn't let her. Said they were saving the last seat. Surprise, surprise, no one ever turned up to sit in it.

Fuck's sake. They're terrified of you guys.

Honestly. Stein would let anyone into her house that had half an excuse to be there, but they can't even talk to the young ones in case their brain cells get frazzled.

They're probably scared you'll all usurp them. Bet your keynote freaked them out.

Yeah, I did actually get into an argument with Warthog after dinner. Undid some of my work with him.

Jesus, what happened? Tell me it wasn't a dispute over a word in a manuscript?

I mean . . .

Does he think it says 'claw' while you think it's 'dark'? And how

could it say 'dark' when it so obviously says 'claw', of course it's
'claw', the vignette was about a crab which really was about a
vagina yes but 'dark' doesn't scuttle does it, you must be insane
boy to really think that.

You are born to be an academic; it almost kills me, or have I killed
you? Corrupted you, definitely, if you can talk like that. Can you
fill in for me?

If you pay me. What was the argument really?

Oh the usual, he thinks we shouldn't talk about Stein's sexuality
and that it shouldn't be relevant, he thinks we should just ignore
that side of her life when discussing her writing.

Seems counter-intuitive?

I mean, the worst part is I agree that we get bogged down in
it. I wasn't even saying it should be our focus, just that it's not
irrelevant. Anyway, I suppose I snapped a little. And he did not
like that one bit.

Honestly, how any of you get anything done . . .

I know. And two blokes arguing about how relevant a woman
being gay is isn't exactly great either. Particularly when it's not
even the real fight. He's just antsy because he knows I've been
looking at that 'Mrs Reynolds' novel too. He's fighting for that
really—

he breathes down the phone
anyway, none of it matters really,
what's been going on over there?

question designed for space   I hear the expanse
        vague enough that it'll fit anything I want to share
until he asked I had nothing   yet   I say

Do you ever get something stuck in your head?
Not a song, but a word or a phrase?

Not that I can think of, not recently anyway. What are you—

*I'll have it on the record that I'm not insane, but I've had 'death
is a death is a death' going round my head. Mindless exercise
keeping me company.*
That's Stein!
What?
*I love you, and I forgive you for not listening to anything I've
been saying for the last five years.*
I laugh *Go on. I know who Gertrude Stein is. I know you think
she's the best, fizzing mind, all that. I know you're surrounded by
Stein-nuts. So go on.*
Rose is a rose is a rose?
Yes . . . okay
something coming back to me   on its way   not quite arrived
leaving silence for him to explain
*It's become the Stein cliché, Stein-nuts over here would roll their
eyes at quoting it.*
Remind me what it means?
*It's like a language game. You hear 'rose' and you think, petals,
scent, the thing itself, the meaning is already packed within
the word. So you don't need to say 'a rose is red', 'rose' is a rose
already.*
Yes,   yes okay, I do remember that
              I do. Used to try it with different objects
              see which worked, which didn't.

Would wonder, could he think 'Rosa' and
get what he needed without anything else.

Maybe you're trying to make sense of it, hey? Tell me to stop if
this isn't helpful.

No, I like this, don't stop. My brain enjoys a close read from you,
carry on.

I hear his smile in his voice. *Well*, he says, *if you're sure.*

Very sure.

You're sitting comfortably?

Extremely comfortable.

Well then. Each time you say 'rose' you unlock the same thing. Just
because it repeats, doesn't mean you get further away. Is it, do
you think, a way of emphasising what's happened? Your brain,
making it real.

Kind of. Yes, I mean, it's like my head is trying to crack what it
is but is never hitting on anything. 'Rose' might tell you rose, but
'death' doesn't, the word is blank.

I'm sorry, Ro. It's difficult. But maybe 'rose is a rose' just doesn't
work with the bigger things? When you say it with death, maybe
rather than working it out, or proving its meaning, you're, I don't
know, stamping it down: containing it. I'm not sure it's even
right, that a death is a death
if only for a little while   it's everything?

itching at my eyes   I know he understands   yet   guilt
I don't think I was there enough for you with your dad,   I say.
You were, you were, love, you were what you could be, and what
I could take in then
but with that stuff   it's hard to share

maybe you feel that already   it's
well   hard to push down into a sentence is what it is
but what I can say is that I'm here for you   whenever
and I understand it isn't an easy feeling,
and that it's hard to know what's going on, really
but I'm here when you want to talk

                    when I want to admit that I regret?
is that what he is saying
            when I want to admit that I wish I had tried?

He pivots   *Have you answered your mum's phone calls yet?*
Not exactly, I say

                    I don't know why but
                    I don't want to mention Mum
                    her having been here   it doesn't
                    I hate the thought of how it went.
Spoken to both of them, though. They're pretty upset, obviously,
I, I find it hard to know what to say to them. Or maybe it's the
other way round, they don't know what to say to me.
It must be difficult, you all had such different relationships with
him too, sounded like it, anyway.
We did, yeah. I mean seriously, what are you even meant to say
when something like this happens?
I was reading the Sue Ryder advice earlier and all it says is,
basically, Don't evoke God.
Cheers Sue.
I texted your dad yesterday, just to send him my love and stuff.
Made me realise I genuinely don't have your mum's phone
number.

Well, lucky you. Don't worry about her.
She'd probably be confused as to who 'John' was anyway.
She actually asked about you earlier!   Oops
We were texting this morning   not a lie
That's good. Your dad always made it sound like she had been
your brother's saviour.
Yeah, she was a bit. I don't know how she's going to deal with it
to be honest.
She'll be okay. She's got Brian. She's got you if you want.
Yeah,
have you seen Christine?
He laughs   so welcome that I smile
            on the phone I realise it's all I want to achieve
a sign we're beyond formality
            that I can still make him emit that unforced peal.
Honestly, Rosa, I get off the train and who do you think the first
person is I see, loitering outside WH Smith's?
I laugh to say I love you
and he says it back as if I really said it
I love you, sweetheart.
You too,
more than a million Christines can,   I say,
so you remember that when she's outside your door at 3 a.m.

We say goodbye and for a minute   there is a magic delay
where I am nothing other than that love
soaked in it.

But then the radiator clicks and my pulse kicks up its pace beating against my skin.

Must not stay still.

Yesterday's stripped sheets and cases are still balled on the floor. I wrap them against my chest.
Be sensible. Practical. Wash.

As I reach for the washing powder under the sink
                                    routine arm-stretch
I see shards of white in the bin
that broken plate gently ushered there by Mum
                            when did that break?
                            Try and reason
                            conceive of an explanation
somehow   I am to blame   I cannot say how or when
but I can say   yes   I am to blame

That has always been the rule
                        even when there were other suspects
            if all else fails
            you're to blame

not even a rule, not really
                                        a fact
                                        a starting place

219

I told John about trap logic
your brother says you exaggerate
then suddenly that's the lens
Drama Queen says this
you're caught

we judge by how action connects back
only ever what consolidates

        Yeah, he said, stroking the ridge of my hip
        not realising, I don't think, just stroking

        I know that well, he said.

But part of me, in having spoken
admitted him into the dynamic

When he met my Mum   I played out his analysis
                like a neurotic commentary
so she was difficult, blind to people?
                I saw him study, scan, conclude:
                seems alright to me

and of course she did   she was,   is

There is so much I don't think about.

Mornings when she would send those texts, written like

fortune cookie missives or you-go-girl horoscope scraps.

Texts like: **I think today is going to be a good day
for you. That blue sky doesn't come out
for nothing.**

Texts like: **Just thinking about my beautiful daughter
and how proud I am of her.**

Texts like: **We're going to have a barbecue this weekend.
What would you like to add to the menu?
Brian wants chicken skewers but I think we
can do better than that. Would you like to
bring Alice? Your brother can stay at home
and revise all he wants but us girls are
going to have some fun.**

Texts like: **Not that I'm a girl. Reading that back I
sound like I should be holding pom-poms.
Love you, sweetheart. Have a nice day at
school. Xxx**

So easy to hear her voice, to hear her phrasings in my head.
Why else would that be other than that she was there. Why
else would that be other than that she was trying, always, to
be present, even when she couldn't be.
And wasn't it fun, that weekend?

Mum had enveloped me and Alice in a hug at the station

wide smile   red-painted toenails poking through her sandals
it wasn't even summer yet but that day had conspired to
pretend: sky overdosed on blue, the smell of blossom strong
as if it were being cooked by the sun.

I had replied to her barbecue text:

> **Haven't got an official name for it yet**
> **but imagine: marshmallows in foil,**
> **maybe some chocolate in there.**
> **Starter, not dessert.**

I've got our starter going, she said,
as she turned off the ignition   and we closed car doors
that satisfying smack of rubber in grooves

There were foil parcels, sitting squat on the grill
Brian standing placid nearby with a spatula

Mallow du Chocolat,
she announced in a horrible French accent
                          as she pulled back the wrapping
                          to a mess of molten goo
Served on a bed of Ice Cream de Vanilla.

That wasn't unusual, was it . . . her effort
                                    her attention to detail
What happened to all of that?

Remember how afterwards Alice said

                              (picking at her split ends)
                              (knees against the train table)
Your mum is so great.

Yeah she's alright isn't she, I said.

                              And Alice slapped her hand down
                              on mine, where it sat on the table
                              slap,   slap,   slap.

No, she said, she's great. Do you know how many times me
and my mum have talked about boys or bras or the right way
to dry your hair?

I said nothing, waiting for the answer.
                    That was normal stuff.
                    All we'd done was speak about normal stuff.

It's zero, she said.

But your mum is so chill!!, I said. She's seen you smoke and
stuff, and always lets me crash.

I know. It doesn't make sense.
But Mum clams when it's just us,
                              Alice blew on the tips of her hair
                                     trying to stay casual.
the closest she has got is saying
'Stay away from tampons'

after I started my period.

I'm sorry, Al, I thought she was cool.

Nope. That's yours, she said,
landing a dramatic prod on the back of my hand.

Remember that.   Conjure that.

But I don't, not often.
Can't even remember what we spoke about, not in full. Brian
had gone back indoors and was watching golf or cricket or
rugby, something none of us pretended to care about, only
knowing it took him away.
We lay on the grass. Giggly and lazy. It seemed as simple
as a chat with Mum. But even then I could have admitted
the feeling. I knew it. She made me feel special in times like
that; precious, that was the feeling. It fed me an undercurrent
of strength. Still have it in me now. I know that, yes, should
allow myself that knowledge. What she gave me.

But it doesn't fit, not with how the rest is painted.

We all need roles   I need them to stick to theirs
or how to make sense?
It's not that I can't forgive   this isn't a simple exchange.

How can I forgive those who don't know they need

forgiveness, who want resolution but don't see why it remains
unresolved?

how can I forgive when one of them is dead?

when my brother stood on my doorstep   facing up

ready to say what I will now never hear

if he is not a monster
then

wouldn't he have been a haven for Alice?
he would have been something, wouldn't he?

Inexplicable to me, but of course it would be
not difficult, not really, to imagine

even those texts from Dylan, that – what? one night? – then
those few other stolen encounters, by the school field
                                        outside the staffroom
I remember those even now, I remember them as something,
as having had effect
even though it wasn't anything, not really, no, but it took me
somewhere else   made me into someone else

construction of another life, all of it a potential

suggestion of an alternative   yes, I can imagine
if she was still here, had the years, had all that distance, now
it would just be a silly flicker in the past
the hilarity of what had once felt real: to have attached so
much to him, to have succumbed, to have felt powerless in
that feeling, that headiness of being lost to someone, the
heat of it, consuming everything, willingly blind to the ill
match, to criticism

unable to acknowledge that they're not worth it, that they are
causing pain that is not worth it, that they are not worth me

but later thinking what? how? what the hell was that?
impossible to resist then, to pull away, it seemed like that,
in not loving myself then   just as Alice somehow couldn't
the control, worth, was in the hands of people I didn't even
respect, didn't like, not even sometimes fancy, yet it was still
theirs, still waiting on some final judgement
still hoping for some final affirmation; to be changed by
them, that was what it was, that their opinion might change
me or change something, that they would grant me some
status I was unable to grant myself

if that is what he was for her,
then yes, I can imagine it.

Check trains.
Check the weather.
Lay out clothes,

make sure my mac is on the back of the door.

I am prepared, physically
only sleep now   only sleep

don't ask the questions already rising

            am I okay?   no, don't answer that
or   what will you say?
     what will she be like? how are you going to handle this?
           how are you going to talk to her?

      why are you not telling John what is going on?
                      no, don't answer those

I try and be efficient. Sitting on the end of the bed,
pressing the soles of my feet on top of a pair of John's trainers.

          Speak soon, I text Dad.
          Speak soon, I text Mum.
          Night x, I text John.

Sunday

It was light (just) when John woke me
and said,   Listen.

There was a woman singing on the street below our window
like a lullaby   subdued, warm

          What the fuck is she doing? I asked
          making a spyhole through the curtains.
          He joined me and we watched her sing
          phone cradled to her ear.

I imagined the song transported, turned tinny

          Who do you reckon she's singing to?
          Fuck knows, he said, pulling me close
          her lover, her son, her needy dachshund,
          fuck knows, he said, but someone – and us.

Someone, somewhere, was soothed by that voice
so I allowed myself to be soothed too   in his arms, her singing

warm in bed   swayed by it   then
can almost feel it again   now

half-remembered   easing   lets me drift
how John stroked my cheek
aligning our bodies   half   asleep

caught almost   back in the memory   held by it

                              held by what we heard
          drifting to that   held by each other

                                   cartwheeling further down
               how she sang   soft   high
as if it were by our ear yet simultaneously   at a great distance

        light   (just)
stirring
                         something pushing against me
stirring
                         sensing a weight by my knees

is that?   bulk in the dark

hand?   against my leg

                         Easy now
                         Just checking you were okay
no
weight easing   cartwheeling on
shadow higher   then gone

falling back already, not real, surely, back to

Wake up,   says my brother (dead)
No,   I reply   (awake)

Wake up,   telling myself
Wake up, wake up, wake up.

                Dazed head
                like I have borrowed someone else's.

Clothes on the floor, coat hung up. Ready for me.

                Let's go.

I'm picking up Jack tomorrow.
Dad had said it as if I would understand perfectly, as if, yes,
I was on fond terms with Jack, knew much about him, knew
where he was and where he'd need picking up from, oh yes,
this would all make sense, I was completely up to date with
Jack's schedule.

And are you dropping in on Jeremy on your way home?
Eh? Who's Jeremy?
Exactly. You first. Jack?
The puppy I'm picking up tomorrow! My puppy,
I've settled on 'Jack'.   (Dad's feet were on the table,
                                      mine tucked under me)
I'm surprised you haven't chosen 'Rosa'. You know it's sexist,
Dad, your daughter going to uni and you getting a dog to
replace her.

That's not what I'm doing . . . you cheeky mutt.

> Little Jack (clocking later)
> as a Jack Russell,
> was also essentially named Dog.

Broke my heart, really   several times over
could hardly say   Can't you get a girlfriend, Dad,
                    don't you want to put your effort
                    into that?

could hardly say it, no, but when the home phone rang
and I picked it up to my brother,
I said: Dad's in love with a dog.
before I passed the phone.

> He put the phone to his ear, listening
> Typical, he said to my brother
> then handed it back to me.
> It's for you, not me, he wants to
> speak to you.

> Oh.
I took the phone.   Just wanted to say good luck,
                    uni tomorrow, right?
                    Yeah, that's right. Thanks.

What was this?   I didn't know how to respond
he had thought of me, and called

234

it wasn't much, yet it felt like a shock

It was a Sunday
I remember that
because I had an image of him
shirt against the ironing board,   phone to his ear.

I ended the conversation before it had even really begun.
I had to.

He had said,   Proud of you, sis, it's exciting.
proud? why did that make me bristle?
but instead, I said,   I've got to go finish packing,
install a lock so the dog doesn't steal
my room, find Dad's vodka stash,
all that, I'll pass you back to Dad.
Okay, he said,
I actually might be in London for a
work thing soon. Next week I think,
I'll text you.
Okay, I said. Bye.

I buy a ticket for the 10:18 to Portsmouth Harbour.

Waterloo is freezing, channels of wind working their way
around me like late passengers. Everywhere is cold. I walk
around Foyles, trying behind shelves

(Is it warmer here?)

twenty-five minutes is little time
but when you are waiting for a train to meet the girlfriend of
your dead brother   then twenty-five minutes is
not little, no, twenty-five minutes is a wide, gaping expanse.

I move back out of Foyles (no difference in temperature) and
check the screens

Platform 13
10:18 flash   **expected 10:24**

I can feel the cold making its way inside: my teeth are stern
against my jaw, keeping my face from slipping. I need to
tell John I'm fine but the energy to send a text is too much.
What would I say? Besides, the cold has reached my fingers
now. They're stiff, unwilling. Later.

The phone made it easier, once   once
a relief   no need for eye contact,
so I could say: Mum, I've started my period
hanging over the side of the bed like I'd seen girls in films
finger through the cord of the landline   gossiping
Don't tell me that I'm going to have to tell Dad as well as you.

Only my line sticks
(repeating it as the phone rang)
Mum, I've started my period
                    Mum, I've started my period

Someone must have told Dad   her or me
otherwise he wouldn't have under-armed sanitary towels
into the trolley, pretending the gesture was nothing

      It's good of you to not be ashamed, Dad,
      many men would cower at suddenly growing a vagina.
      Loud and proud, Rosa,
      I'm hoping my breasts follow next week
      his grin thick with something else
            me, too, caught in a squirm

            I was growing breasts then, after all
            too subtle for him to have noticed yet
            my secret, I was sure

How was he going to deal with this?
Then, that was the question laced through it all.
Now, I'm not so sure. Was it not only a longing? For Mum
to have been the one? Even though she was she was she was,
she was always able to take things in hand, a phone call, a
train ride away, it seemed like an eternity
                but wasn't it every weekend?
                she hardly disappeared
Was it even to do with that, wasn't it purely the contrast
the choice of it, the divergence from what was

            (can it be that simple?)

Clatter behind, routine, as the train begins to move.

A door has lost its electricity. Guided by the motion of
the train: whacking, whacking, enough to break an arm, a
collarbone, five fingers, whatever got in its way.

What am I doing? Thwack. What am I doing? Thwack.

The question reaches into my head, draws itself between
phrases. I am cold (what am I doing?) my brother is dead
(what am I doing?)

Mrs Clark arrives. Train-window exercise.
Uninvited, irrelevant, yet easy to conjure.

Mrs Clark
This is the point where you seek reassurance.
You want me to say, You are special
that you were the student who stood out
who was always going to be something

But I'm not going to say that   no chance
and not because I'm trying to keep you modest
it's simply not true.

Okay, but I wasn't asking you to
and I'm not fifteen any more,
I don't care

Mrs Clark
You don't care?

It would be sad if I was still harbouring a need to hear that
my old teacher Mrs Clark thought well of me, that dear Mrs
Clark who I haven't seen in years thinks I'm special

Mrs Clark's son
I think you're special

Mrs Clark
Toby, get back to your room

Hey, Toby, what's your favourite song?

Mrs Clark's son
Why?

Is it 'Who Let the Dogs Out'?

Mrs Clark
We're leaving now

Rain heavy against the window
pulling me out   thwacking door
train, you're on the train

stuck in a sleepwalk
whose head is this?

                        Nice doughnuts.
                        Brian clutching them
                        like a knock-off Pied Piper.

My brother only needed to say Nice doughnuts.

Brian looked from his doughnuts and back
                        more a child than us
                        caught in the disappointment

a delay before he laughed   I had already been set off
a stiff Ha ha

You can have one if you want? he said
as if they weren't for us in the first place.

We wouldn't want to deprive you.
My brother was in his element
though stopping before he had really started.

Mum back, clutching her purse and a car park ticket.
And how are we all getting on? she asked,
as she leant her arm to push the slip onto the dashboard
the back of her head fielding the windscreen.

Just lovely, my brother said,
so good to finally meet Doughnut Man.
                        Doughnut Man. She almost mouthed it

They start by causing trouble, she said to Doughnut Man,
then loosen up. It's all part of the performance.

I didn't realise you knew us so well.

Well I am your mother.

I bent my fingers into speech marks,
Doughnut Man is more of a mother.
When have you ever bought us doughnuts?

She sprawled a hand on top of each of our heads,
pulling us towards her shoulders   grinning at Brian
Mad to believe they're related to me.

                        they shared the grin
Us and doughnuts waiting for it to pass
until we wriggled away, grabbing the bag out of his hand.
Cellophane, sugar. Fuck that, he said, or I said, fuck that.

                        Lulling in the movement.
Landscapes flashing like suggestions.

        Bacon up close is not pink, not really
        holographic like the scales of a fish
        turning yellow, blue, purple

        I'm surprised you didn't eat it, he said
        after the maggot I figured anything
        was up for grabs

that was different
I didn't mean

Two men fishing near where we were camping
stench of something I didn't understand
a man addressing me   annoyed as I retorted
small girl hair wet to her forehead

You've got a big mouth
he said   do you never shut up?
It was a fight   I knew that   understood that
one of us had to win

Something about the sureness, the smugness of him
meant it was a fight I had to win.

His friend chuckled as an ice cream container appeared
I nudged my nose over the side
saw little yellowed moving things

they were so tiny

Let's eat, he said.

Yes of course I did   still   I know   of course I did
there was no choice   jag of rock sharp against my bum
                        as I dangled the wriggling body
            man too   swinging it above his mouth

strange reddish coating dusting their bodies

Eat it   his grin enough, him still hovering
Fine
slow-motion chewed and chewed and chewed to fairy dust.

Fake lip-smacking then horror
the man pulling his maggot from the other side of his face,
                                right where it had been hidden

You didn't actually, did you?
                                        Of course I did
hands empty   in front of me

brother silent   then running   to no one just away
Of course I did
                                thought I was going to die
lying in the tent that night
sure there wouldn't be a next morning
                                sweet stupid little girl

Woman near me now,
with her early egg-and-cress sandwich
wouldn't want to know about the maggot   no   no   no
                pulling the crust from her mouth in disgust
                mulched egg diving from her lips
                making a home on the train carpet

hard to explain, hard to make it sound like anything other

than what it was yet wasn't

haphazard memories   why should any of it make sense
why should any of it fit
nothing more than haphazard memories

                                         out of place
unsewn   hearing barking
on this train   now   barking   and
for a breath
I expect Dad and the bloody dog
                        him to be walking down the train aisle
                        What on earth are you going to say to
                        this poor woman?
                        What are you going to say to her?
Who, what, Dad?   Julia, what are you going to say to her?

but no   of course   not him.

As I reach the right street, I practise her name out loud
                          Julia
trying it on for size   transgression on my tongue
but it's nothing
                          Julia
Julia!   what of it

I am counting   7

                 9

                                        11
to find out   what?   13
                                              15
                                                    17
                              21
this is it   25
                                          red door
already, I am learning something
                                          red door

superfluous, maybe, but   something

This was the door he slammed, locked
said,   Thanks, mate   as he accepted a parcel
That once he would have looked at   perhaps on first meeting
and thought   Too red! Sore thumb of an entrance.

But now   no   Sunday, Wednesday
four days ago he would have just seen his door, there you are

He closed this door four days ago as casually as ever
no thought, no recognition   that it was anything other
than the same refrain
no finality, no last look

none of that   closed it
unknown   no hint his sister would be outside of it on Sunday
hesitant
                        just as he was at mine

when I said No
when I said No, sorry, no
and shut him out

I hadn't thought, on the train
that it was same journey he had taken (backwards) to see me
did he hover at my door? taking a deep breath?
preparing himself like I am now, hand not yet raised to the bell

I count down
the door, my arm, my legs on this step are absurd

                              none of this is happening

how am I here?   Forcing my finger high.
                              A prod away from the doorbell.
Simple action, this.   A second away.
On the threshold, one move left, yet everything is contained
in this, none of it has meant this, not really, all of it could be
anything. But now: no buffer, last delay
all of me stiffened   he can't be here
preparing for an apprehension, a change, but really

                              undemanding
                              manageable

A small task.
Think only of that.
Just   (one second away)
buzz   (prod)

Rosa   you must be Rosa   jesus
you are so much like him look at you.

Her mouth twists
tears falling down their set paths
cheeks patched pink   *Sorry*, she says
                      this must be difficult for you too
                      and here I am, sucking at the air.

Walking through the hallway
I am confronted by
a man's coat near the door, modest brown
one pair of keys on a two-rung rack

Let's have a cup of tea in the kitchen
                              plates and mugs by the sink,
               a chopping board sloped against the side

it's only a picture of them on the fridge
that I avert from

                              too bright

I mean to look but my eyes refuse   warning me away
so I don't   not directly   only enough to know
                                       grass, arms, teeth

So this is him
so this was him.

Have you been here for a while? I ask.
Six months or so. We wanted somewhere
bigger, more space, a garden.

Lovely, I go to say, but don't. It isn't lovely.
A garden isn't lovely if her boyfriend's dead.

I cycle through words, but nothing

It was good of you to text me, she says,
I didn't think I'd ever get to meet you,
it can't have been easy   she extends the word
                    moulding it into a question.
                    Into something to be answered.

A text, a train, that's all.

                    Ladies and gentlemen,
                    Rosa begins!
                    Put your seat belts on,
                    the bitch is accelerating.
Okay. Stop. Check myself.

Tea?   she asks.   *Yes please.*
She clicks the kettle, takes mugs from the cupboard, milk
from the fridge. Pincers two teabags from a nearly empty jar.
So, how did you meet?   (the kettle hisses)
Oh. I love telling this story. Did. Maybe still will, I don't know.
He was sitting in my seat on the train   (the kettle calms)

I had a reservation and the train was busy so I said
That's my seat!
Well thank you, it's very comfortable, he said. Cheeky bastard.
Did he give it you back?
Yes of course, he was only joking   can't tell if her voice flits
but later,   harsh or if I only imagine it
we got off at the same stop
smirked at each other
then realised we were walking the same way
fireworks, et cetera.

She ripples her hand in a theatrical gesture. A sarcastic ta-da.
(Ending spoilt)

Ah.

She sets our tea down in smart red mugs   *Thanks.*

My friend just left, after giving me a hug and a lasagne. They've assigned themselves some kind of rota. Which is very sweet, of course. And I guess they did know him. But it's not theirs, you know? It's theoretical for them. Maybe that's unfair but it's nice to see someone who definitely gets it. Your mum and dad have both been in contact too, so that's nice. I don't know. Is anything nice, probably not.

No, there's not much niceness to it. Are you managing okay?
Work gave me the week off, but I'm going to go back in tomorrow.
Too much sitting around.

We can stand up if you want?
She laughs   then brings her mouth back to still
ready to ask,
How are you doing?
I'm alright.   she pushes up her eyebrows
                              her forehead wrinkling in the effort

You look knackered, Rosa, like a ghost.
I know he tried to talk to you. It must be   a weird
strange thing to—

Mum said that as well, that he was going to speak to me,
I smile to try and sweeten   aware my words are strict
. . . hard to know what to say about it,   unrelenting
I didn't know it was the last chance.
hardly came here to talk about regret   don't want to,
what good does it do, bitterness clinging, like coffee on teeth

She looks down at her mug   *Hmmm*   she says
I'm not sure how happy this milk is   *I'll be honest,*
it did go off yesterday   or maybe the day before that actually.

Don't get me wrong, I say   little clumps on the surface
I didn't come here to attack your tea-making,
but I'm probably not going to drink this.
She squeezes her shoulders up in a little shudder
No you will not,   *let's try this again*
reversing back up with the mugs, back up to standing,
back to sink   *I've got wine?*

maybe that's more appropriate anyway . . .
                              looking to me for approval

Definitely something I can get behind.
I think I would have said yes to anything

Great
kitchen fussing   peal of glasses   familiar glugging pour

background   as I examine   next
the fronds of a spider plant   almost tickling the tabletop
waxy to the touch
strange domestic scene   he was here, ate toast in this kitchen
                                        sat in this chair
calm,   there's a calm that disturbs me
                        how would he have managed here?

This is better, she says, as she passes me my glass
                              dark, promising red
                              mine large, hers tentative
Thank you   quiet for a moment,
                    noticing her cheekbones
                    caverns as she takes a sip   eyes pronounced
                                        lidded and wide
didn't notice, not at first   had to examine
the kind of pretty emphasised by looking
                    aware all at once
                    of how little I've looked in the mirror

You look so much like him, she says, like a mirror talking back
                          studying just as I have been
sorry, I know I've already said that,
but I'm just getting used to it.

I've never really noticed, I say,
I guess it's probably hard to see.

It's nice   I'm not . . . don't think I'm freaking out or anything
it's a bit of a gift to be honest.
I smile   trying not to fidget   not to feel the charge of her gaze
                          of her using my face to see him
don't like how I could be twinned with him like that
                          not under my control
wanting to push against somehow
force a split

Did he ever   can't help myself
drive you insane?   staked in me
                                       making me ask it
She splays her hands, checking her joints, swivelling her
mouth in delay.
Sorry. Not entirely sure why I asked that.
Came from deep down, by the sound of it,
I know your relationship wasn't simple,
though as we're only meeting now he's gone,
                          she pauses as she hears herself
that much would be easy to guess.

It's a strong voice. A kind of strong that implies the opposite.
She is talking with force to keep herself here   in this moment
not to lose it to what has passed

she pats her chest as if in acknowledgement of what she is
concealing

                    it takes me out that pat
                    John so often
                    rather than saying I love you
                    would pat his chest   tap tap
                    as if there was something inside of him
                    building
                    that he wanted to draw attention to

                        Why do I think that in past tense?

he would do it right now   if he were here
although
he may have some distractions
shaking his head to clear the confusion
like a dog out of the bath
he may have some questions,   like
Why aren't you replying to me? Who is she?
Are you okay?
but once that was done   after the make-up, the consolation
yes, he'd tap   tap tap
and tell me   in that gesture   that he loves me

he told me once   didn't he   how it unsettled him
that he had said I love you to others in the past
each time, thinking afterwards, that wasn't right
but at the time sure he did

trying to be romantic
but I heard it like a warning
you are only safe now

love can unstick
you can't even trust it as a memory

how to phrase   surely, she knows
another way
Would you say   I begin to ask   stop
I guess,
I wondered whether you ever thought of him
as an aggressive person?

I am starting to question why you are here,   she says it gently,
as if she is only filling me in on her thought process,
I thought you wanted to meet me.

I did, do, you're his girlfriend of course I do.

She looks at me   no words   I scrutinise
watching her face for a reaction   anything will do
I just feel like I need to hear something of what, I—
He told me,   she says.

He did? He wouldn't what would he say how would he tell?

It's okay,   she says
childhood can be a headfuck,   she says
I think most of us end up doing things we regret
we hardly understand what any of it means
and he forgave you   *he wished,*
he really wished you could've known each other better.

           He forgave me?
What did he say about me?

I'm not saying he made you out to be a villain,
        only giving quiet,
        only giving an expectant pause
what do you want, a full summary? You were just kids. You used
to wind him up, twist him round, knot him, until he lashed out,
and he regretted that. Childhood hung over him, sat on top of
everything, marking its presence. He hated it. He hated, hated,
hated it. I have never seen a man carry so much sadness around
with him.

I would say to him,
just go and see her
she could be thinking the same over there, with no idea. There's no
point wasting time thinking about it, repeating the thoughts, the
feelings, without at least trying.

*The day he went to see you he was nervous but he was energised, I
had drummed it into him, made him see the hope, made him gear
up for something that was going to heal the past, heal you both,
that was going to shoo the fucking regret away, finally, finally,
something was going to happen.*

And I closed the door in his face.

And you closed the door in his face.

You're silly, Alice said
sillier than I thought   school isn't real
once you're out of here you'll have people
at your feet and I'll be some witch in a shed,
waiting for you to come visit me.

You couldn't have known,   Julia says.

No, I couldn't have.   But that hardly makes it better.
                                No justification   not really
hurts   how condensed   all of it   years of insistence
overshadowed by one refusal

Julia speaks into the silence.

Would you like anything?

Silence

a snack?

Silence

a hug?

Silence

for me to stop asking questions?

There is something Alice
            in the way she grins   knowing to keep pushing
until I speak

Sorry   you don't know
it's not

am I here to correct?

Did he ever speak about Alice?
                        Yes,   she says   *so sad,*
tears are back
                        tragedy fucking followed him around

god I can't believe it.

Me neither,   I say   *me neither.*
She was my friend, did he tell you that?

Julia looks at me
No, I didn't realise, she says,
picking at the side of a finger with her thumb.

I know we were kids,   I hear myself, I know, I know
so what does that mean, and it seems possessive too,
or something, 'She was MY friend', but she was.
He fucked her up, did he tell you that?

From what he said, and I can't remember all of it, you know, it
was an old thing, a sad thing, but an old thing, but it sounded
like he tried so hard with her, and he was a kid too.

She leans back   stretches her hand across her stomach
                                            curved presence
                        not a bump   a thickness
I almost don't   but she meets my eyes with directness
                        saying yes,   you can ask
You're?   I say
Nod, first.
Then
Five months, she says.

I,

I came here to tell you—
I came here to tell her the story of my brother
but I can no longer understand why.

A baby
I don't want to think about it

Better without him
Better without him   surely   better without him

Do you know if it's a boy or a girl?
I ask, trying to ask the questions
trying to be good

The mother hates the baby before the baby even knows it has
a mother

        that line comes with me everywhere

Girl,   she says   and I feel   relief
relief that sends me forward, that turns my eyes hot.
A girl,   is all I can say.
I do not recognise my voice
there is nothing much any more I recognise

        You look like that   my brother used to explain

because she would hit her stomach
when you were inside
trying to empty herself

Mum didn't know how to make you leave so she'd hit, hit, hit
                                      and hope
I'd see her   he'd say   swollen
screaming   he'd say   for you to get out

Enough, enough, enough, she'd scream
                              desperate

It's not that I believed him   not for ever
initially, yes, but not for ever

I shouted at Mum in a row that blurs with the rest
almost teenage

I'm so sorry your accidental baby isn't behaving how you'd
like her to.

        What are you on about? You weren't an accident.

Julia touches my hand   warm, clammy against mine

Can I show you something?
Sure   curiosity sticks the word in my throat
following her path out of the kitchen further into the house
       pregnant   I say to her back   perfectly silent

pregnant,   pregnant,   pregnant,
        into their bedroom
blue-and-white-striped duvet
        instantly clear whose side is whose
one bedside table with a necklace coiled on top of a paperback
half-emptied hand cream standing to attention
the other   his
where she lingers, waiting   radio and nothing else
        except
Your handiwork, I believe,   she says
        scrap of paper above the radio

        yellow-patched
        network of creases
he had it Blu-Tacked to the wall in our last place too.

God I don't even remember doing that
and I don't, but it's unmistakable, unmistakably mine
        sugar doughnut with eyes and mouth
        speared on a stickman body

        Doughnut Man.

Poor guy, she says, *he was doomed to a nickname that stuck
between the two of you.*

He can't have . . . had this up   listen to me,
        pathetically trailing off
Well I hardly did it, she says   teasingly

studying me with her arms crossed
stomach rounding under

half-familiar
how I'd drawn his eyebrows in an evil downward slant
jam spot on top   it's me, yes
how I'd do it   yes
but I don't know when how old how long he must have had it

Softie,   I say
can hardly word much more

and she smiles   sneaking her arm around my shoulder

back of my eyes fidgeting

I don't know how you're handling it, Julia.   I manage that much.
Oh I hardly am, really
it's just about the worst thing that could happen,
just about the worst

she breathes out of her mouth, loud

this is a reassurance though   gentle pat
in its own strange way.
Have you got a name?   I mean, had you discussed?
Not yet no, nothing settled. We mainly just called her Bean,
that was how she looked on the ultrasound, like a little bean, all
curled up.

Sweet,   I say

                    that's sweet.

                    You needed so much of me, you two.
I don't know when   but she said it   Mum
                    she did

Do you know how exhausting it is, to be stretched like that?
There was never enough of me.

Yet Mum was always able to tickle him into something
upturned
into an admission   a compromise   a grin
she would prise it from him

just like with Alice

studying them   when they were together
                     in school
sitting at lunch

sometimes saying nothing   stabbing chips with their forks
but other times   other times   squealing!
Alice could   both of them somehow knew

warmth   under my breastbone   highs of my cheeks
wine snaking its way through me

I've taken up enough of your day, I say   looking at my phone
I should head.   as if clocking the time
You're welcome to stay,
we could get some food or something.
No, I should go. Thanks though. I'm booked on the next train,
I'll—   I don't know how to finish this.

You've got my number if you want to talk,
she opens the door   begins to,
pausing   fingers tilted on the latch
ajar,   not broad enough for me to fit
it means so much that you came to see me.
She halts.
There was something I was going to mention, she says.
Maybe it's wrong to. I don't know.
What? I ask
She twists the latch back and forth. I know. Somehow, I know.
Did you think it was?   I say.   No.
That he meant to?

I don't know, she says, *I don't know. I wouldn't have—*
he was down, yes, but I hadn't been worrying that he was going
to or anything like that.

Then why—

One of our first dates, she says. Quicker. *When we were starting*
to feel close, get the pace of each other, we started throwing

random questions at each other, you know in the way you do,
because it's entertaining and it allows you to be unpredictable,
to find jokes, hear unexpected things. And I asked – it sounds
macabre, but there was a warm-up, there really was: 'What
would your death row meal be?', something like that, and after
that, I asked – 'If you were going to kill yourself, how would you
do it?' It sounds ridiculous, why the hell would I ask that, I wish
that I fucking hadn't, but it just did, it happened.

Car crash.

I don't need to ask but I do.
What did he say?   My voice someone else's. Cold, single note.
He said he'd turn the car, or whatever else. He liked the drama of
it. As big as death. I gave some arsey response: That might not kill
you. Would be embarrassing to survive, something like that. And
he said, 'I'd make it work.' I remember that because I believed
him. Yes, he'd know somehow. He'd make it work.
Jesus. *Jesus.*

I shouldn't have told you.
Nod, swallow
swallowing down what, I don't know,
something not yet worded

You don't know, I say. *Really, Julia, you don't.*
No, I don't, she says. *But there'll always be that question mark.*
He loved you, I say, *you have a child coming. It's a horrible*
coincidence but you can't punish yourself for that. I'm glad you

told me because in turn I can tell you: No. Don't believe this. Don't let this rewrite what you know. Don't lose him in the process, or yourself, or what you had.

Thank you, she says. *You're right. I'm just scared, and it would be the worst, the worst of anything, so I can't help but think it.* She closes her eyes. Then reopens. Smiles, just a little. *Why don't you give me a hug*, I say. She squeezes my waist, face on my shoulder. The ridiculousness of us, suddenly, in this corridor. On the threshold. That it's now, here, that she shares this.

You should go, your train.
No, it doesn't matter. I can stay.
It's fine, please, I just needed to speak it. I don't believe it so much now I've said it.
I'm glad I came, I say. Hoarse.
Me too, she says.

Last time we spoke   before the gap   before the end
before the no sorry no   the decider   that last time

it was me   my botched attempt
     I did try   once   didn't I?
out of university   and   honestly, sad
     honestly, sick
sick,
at the idea of having a brother yet having nothing to say for

it, knowing nothing of him, of what it even meant for us to
be siblings

sick of it, and sad, and wondering
what was the harm, really?

hovering over his name in my contacts
right there   easy
simple as a double tap

once, onto his name
once, onto the number

Rosa, he had said when he picked up
       shocked, curious, quiet.

I can't remember what I said how I organised the words
but we arranged to meet that Sunday
he suggested London, knowing I was there
and then

     there he was

the shock of that encounter   of how easy it was
a phone call, and then in front of each other

It was faltering, I remember, stop-and-start
I cried almost immediately

and he looked at the ground while I cleared my face

knowing I didn't want him part of that
knowing I didn't want to start like that

we walked   side by side   through Green Park

past tourists with their hired deckchairs in the bitter April
past a woman with her legs wrapped around a man's waist
giggling into each other's mouths
                          my brother raising an eyebrow to me
                          in jaunty acknowledgement

We must have caught up, reconciled at least a little,
I know I was glad
it was good to see him
and I was surprised   I knew that
enough that I thought I could broach   that we could talk
enough that I had said

                          You know you used to terrify me?

Is that what I said?   scared me?   that I was scared of you?
You know   (I know, that I carried on)
you weren't exactly a great brother to me growing up.

The stop,   there it was
          The turn,   there it was

Rosa, he said.　　　　　Furious　　　　he looked furious
　　　　　　　　　but landing his words carefully

Would you take a moment,　he said,　to look at this mark,
this scar I have had as decoration on my face for, what, seven
years?

That was one—　　　　I said
I'm not trying to sound heartless, I'm not trying to sound
like I don't regret it
but that's one—
　　　　　　　　　　one thing
　　　　　　　　　　I could write a fucking catalogue

I don't recall you ever saying sorry, I'm racking my brain here,
but nope, nothing comes to mind.

Well done, well done for pushing me to hurt you just so
everything before could be erased, past, compared to that
everything else safely before.

Rosa—

Fuck this, I said. This is always how it goes, why did I even,
what did I expect, it doesn't work, it's never going to fucking
work.

He grabbed my arm as I turned to go and I screamed
　　　　　　　　　　white hot on my skin

                              wanting to pull myself out
                                    of my own body
                                    get out, get away
Don't touch me, don't touch me, don't touch me.

He texted the next day:
I hated that, Rosa. I didn't want to upset you.

The day after:
I don't want to upset you any more,
that's not what I want.

I know what I replied exactly
having to summon the sternness
                        the certainty

                        I don't want to talk to you again.
that is what I said

and to be sure, I blocked his number and felt   honestly
                                                     relief
the cleanness of it. Stunningly, easily exact.
Like a straight line drawn in thick ink.

That was the me he knew when he knocked on the door.
The one he must have been anticipating. Six years on.
Blank of time.

He can't have done it, he can't have meant it.

He would never have killed himself.

What do I know, how could I know, yet the certainty
that he wouldn't.   Didn't.

I hate that Julia told me. Yet closer to her for it, that's a
truth.

Even though I was a dick to say, Was he aggressive?
To bring my version of him with me. To go there so quick
too, without thinking of anyone other than him and me, a
dynamic made really only of an impression of an impression,
her him surely more real than mine.

There was nothing
is still nothing
that I know for sure.

He was right to turn up, to try again anyway
he had waited six years, hadn't he?

Brother   that was what I knew
            brother
                        turned into some stone gargoyle
                        eternally baring its teeth at passers-by
even how he was with Alice I didn't know, Mum too. I knew
so little of him.

Was it always death
was that the only way?

I was so sure   of who he was
                                           of what had passed

what else could   splinter that
was this always the only way of learning?
not learning, no, lens shift
hitting the light differently
like spinning a jewel in your hand

the same   yet   that glint

that glint,   never looked like that before

Was death really always the answer?
Surely absurd to have been the only way.

Hardly noticing   shine on the road
my surroundings   umbrellas marshalling people past
quick brushstrokes   a man with a hoodie
                       drawn tight under his chin,
                       face like the heart of a sunflower.

How to make sense?   How to have the conviction
the arrogance   to believe any of it is due some sense
to believe I could force a throughline
                       sharp nail struck through

there's no one to ask
I have hardly   anything

                              shattered
scrabbling around for pieces that won't come

now I've left Julia   what's to say she is real
                              what can be said of any of it?

He can't have. Surely. Always so strong, so him.
He was about to become a father. What would that mean, to
still want to kill yourself. For that to not mean enough.

Can't. Can't let it in.

Dressed in haze.   There'll always be a question mark.
Head closed in, filled in.

But the police would have, if they thought it was suspicious
they would have said something, asked something.

The brother I know wouldn't have but what brother do I
know, what brother do I know
I know a sketch, I know lines on tracing paper.
How long has my brother not been mine?

all of this now   shards   these are the ones I have

I hadn't

Julia having a girl   I hadn't thought
my niece   if I want her to be   she can be
        that would be something   wouldn't it?
but how would I
        remember what I said to him
        not asking for the sake of an answer

Do you think Mum regrets it?

It was a taunt.
I knew he was worried   disturbed by Mum's disappearance
Regrets what?   caught, eyes wide
     Us – having kids – the lot.

Unfairly innocent voice

the taunt is a lesson in resistance
like feeling a new object   push to see what gives
        finding limits

It was only a question   but his face was more
trying to protect me by not saying yes

I hope not, he said.   Funny what we forget.

Why do I never recall his softness?

Then firmer, not for him but for me
Surely not, he said.

At Waterloo, everyone gets off, and I wait
I imagine a train guard stopping
                    Are you okay, miss?
                    You look like you've had a tough day.

In reality, nothing
                    except a woman avoiding my eyes
                    as she pulls the plastic liner from the bin.

What difference is there   between me and my brother?

I went to see her   for what?

who tries to ruin another's life?

no one knew my brother other than me
no one knew him as a son except my dad   sometimes Mum
as a boyfriend, that particular boyfriend, except Julia

stuck
unable to cocoon then split, fly, any of it

still past me, scared me

hitting my fists against any part of him
but like a wall
none of it fucking yielding,
none of the satisfaction you imagine from a punch
nothing giving way   my strength not enough

that was why   cornered   when once more I knew he
would goad me, not letting me leave the house for the fun of
it, laughing at me while I was trapped like a spider under a
glass, just for entertainment, that was how it seemed, hitting
me if I tried to go through the door, pinning me to the
ground. He would pretend to be a prison guard as if we were
only playing an immersive game, as if my pleas were only me
staying true to my role
that was why, once more cornered,
I picked up the gas lighter that sat next to the oven,
clicking it as if to light the hob   then to him, quick
pushing the back of his head forward

                                        as I held the pad
                                        of my finger
                                        numb against the trigger

I don't remember   can't   how long was I
how could I   without him pushing me back, getting me away
I don't understand how it could have been possible
how I had the power to

all I know is that my finger was numb and   shoes on
                                        bag by door

I was prepared, wasn't I, ready to get out

it was a lighter   not an axe
I didn't think beyond that

I only saw a way of making it end   frozen in that
                                                                         suspended
but not meaning to   not really

I felt myself fizzing as I ran, like the flame had reached
within me   smoking my flesh from the inside

I had plans to see Alice and I ran from the house, down the
street, through the field that led to the gate I could climb
over, getting me close to the lake where we had promised to
meet, which I had in my mind like a talisman: a focus point
as I ran, as I escaped home and him, as I ignored how my legs
jellied, it was all with the knowledge that I couldn't say what
had just happened
I couldn't say because it would mean telling all of it
how I'd have to start:
                              I burnt him, picked up the lighter, had a plan
that wouldn't work   I knew
it would position me wrong straight away
I knew, as I ran, terrified he was following
                                              the lake clear in my mind
that I would say nothing

it was the first night I got drunk   properly

                                        not giggling through sips
that fire instilled something   it should have been disturbed
but it wasn't

Alice and I had already selected the evening
we had decided
tonight we were going to get drunk
                                        properly, absolutely, drunk

we were fifteen but men sought any way of making Alice
in debt to them, they went into supermarkets and came out
proffering WKDs, Bacardi Breezers
saying, Something sweet for someone sweet.

There she was, that evening
by the lake just as we had agreed
6:30 for a 6:45 start, she had said, laughing
        something we had heard her mum say on the phone once
        that lodged itself as forever funny

There she was
with a blanket smoothed into a perfect square
protecting us from the dirt that settled on your skin like dust

we arranged the snacks   (we knew we had to go slow,
                                        we were here to do this right)
and we laughed, it was like our birthday, she kept saying so
Happy birthday to us, on a Wednesday, what a Wednesday

I remember that   fleeting power
                                    we only needed each other
                                    that was the feeling

the lighter catching, warming,
as I drank down lava-lamp-coloured liquid

I gulped down more, sensing the fire there, not unpleasant,
it was a charge, a trophy too, because hadn't I won?
I had got out, he was the one screaming
I felt him disappear that night   finally dissolved   settled
me and Alice, so close   him inconsequential
                                            that was what it was
                                            finally, he didn't matter
we talked, seeing ourselves there and ahead
in ten years, I was sure, we would still be doing this, this
freedom, fire down, down, the early taste of what was to come,
as we drank, that's what it was, a promise
my brother didn't matter, none of it did
I could come out with Alice while others would soon
enough be made to go to bed, here we were by the lake that
in the morning parents would be circling, kids taking aim
with bullets of bread, but for now, it was ours

I wish I could remember the night in its entirety
but I only have shards
shards I know too well, know the ridges, how to trace my
finger along the side without cutting the skin

remembering our hope in its entirety would be too much

she was beginning to worry me then   I forget that

forget or bury   scrub over

but she was manic, saying things I couldn't understand, dark
disbelief, her body set to be used, men pushing her, of feeling
nothing, but she was still her, she hadn't lost that, not yet,
and that night she was real, playful, making me laugh until
it was uncomfortable like I had to keep it in or I would die
without preamble – up like a flame

she was sincere too, we spoke about getting out (that we
knew for sure, that we were going to leave), about living
together in Manchester, London, of our lives together
beyond all of this

Then she announced: Dessert!
and we ate our doughnuts, sugar creeping across my lips, her
grinning at the sight

You've got sugar all over your face Four-Eyes, she said.

I didn't tell her off for calling me Four-Eyes, a nickname she
loved to use even though I didn't wear glasses, her insisting it
worked anyway, how during tests I would stroke the bridge
of my nose like I was steadying an imaginary pair, inching
them closer to me and that was enough, apparently that

was more than enough to justify Four-Eyes, no, I didn't tell
her off, usually I would but then I only laughed, and as she
joined in, brushing away sugar with her fingertips
I halted on the edge of my own finger in my lap, at the hot
itch of an emerging blister

                            trace of a secret I didn't want to tell

Later   getting home
grateful to sneak into a quiet house
                        no sign of what had happened as I left
                        no one waiting for me
I switched on the lava lamp propped next to my bed
the blocks of wax bitty, staying put,
but the next day I woke to it hot by my head,
bubbles moving like jellyfish

twelve years since she died   why am I back?   twelve years
I was a teenager, kid, what could I know,
and Alice   jesus christ   a child

I see sixteen-year-olds now and I think: you, it would be you
deciding to kill yourself, how could you even think that, what
would drive that, what could force that into a kid's head?

                    how could my brother be capable?

I had always pinned him as some of the cause
                    but I lived with him

and I didn't ... he was young too

laughing as he stole her chips
heads back grins as wide as faces

he couldn't
      there was nothing to be done, how could I, him, anyone

Placing the words within me   Careful,
strict sentences   I couldn't help her.

But even if I could   Careful!
No, but even if I could, I couldn't blame myself, I was a kid too
it wasn't my responsibility, I wasn't being negligent,
I didn't know what to do, but just because I could have helped
                                    if I could have helped
doesn't mean it was my fault
how could it be his either
how really is any of this to do with him

                              but it's what I have

I knew when Alice died that I couldn't forget
        that I had to replay and replay and replay to have her set
                              every conversation archived

But now my brother is dead, I can't find him.
It isn't the same. Thought it would work the same.
Shards. Just shards. Unreal.

                              Can he have?
                              Would he have?
                              Too much of a mirror
                              Surely, too much of a mirror
What was my brother?

Too late. The stupidity, the complicity, of asking now. Too
late to reinsert, to retake, to attempt to pull him out of where
I've buried him, over and over, like rewinding a tape, back to
that, remembering, detailing, enforcing the grooves.

Can't retell a story.   Know the beats. Know the rhythm.

Basic rule of all of this.   Can't go back.

I stir   a street away from our flat   dehydrated, head aching
like I've accidentally fallen asleep on the sofa

I was on the train, I remember, autopilot taking advantage.

The rain has arrived.
The stoops dark with it. My hands damp shellfish pink.
Nearly home, I tell myself, trying to take control of the journey.
Nearly home.   The streets are quiet. My head too.
                    Silence has never been relief.

Collarbone.   I try only to recall the bone. Suspended.

Shining cold, alone. Not the rest. Not the rope. Not the joke
taken too far. Laugh that pitches to a scream.

A line of water runs from my scalp
past my eye
down the side of my nose
until it hangs on my chin
I put it out with my thumb
and murmur, *nearly home, nearly home, nearly home.*
Not there, no one there, nearly home.

How hard must it be
just to resign from my role as sister
to say, you know what?

The past is past is past is past

but what do I have then?
if I erase my past   pretend   start again
I have nothing more than a routine
is that enough?

(Pretend question)
(Really)
(I must ask)

Is it even possible?

My brother told Alice.
Showed her that new, raw mark by his hairline.
You can't give an ending without a story.
It was never going to get to the heart of it, not even close
but truth was hardly the point.

He told me, Alice said.
He told me. I saw his burn. I saw it, Rosa.
                          What the fuck is wrong with you?
He told her, like it was the start.
Places switched. I was him; he was me.

Always hated how neat it was.

A fixed dot
in the telling

becomes   fly caught with tissue
                              raisin lost in the toss

becomes   first drop of ink
                              blood on a bedsheet
paper cut or insect bite or, more brown than red, no

something else entirely
something I cannot
even recognise

almost nothing fixes
spun constantly from its post

how to pin
almost nothing

never even really knew him
loved him, feared him
couldn't get rid of him

none of that is knowledge
only half-measurements

                        an almost

Home.
Air is restless
saying, something is wrong
up stairs,   no one kitchen
living room,   no one
bathroom door open   (no one)
our bedroom,   no one?

door nearly closed shut
did I leave it like that?   I don't see why I would
inching closer   please, no one

calling out *John?* even though he can't be here

just to have a name to say
I do not live in a horror, remember, these things do not
happen, pushing away the images that tentatively begin
to encroach, no no, pushing back the scenes that like to
escalate, pushing all that away
then, pushing the door
hard against the wall
I scan the corners, make myself walk in, under bed,
behind door, in wardrobe, all of it, look
no one
not even my brother

phone flashes,
stacked with calls, texts   (I should)
Mum and John taking turns to hope for an answer
                                        (should answer)
                                (should stop them worrying)

easier, wouldn't it   if it had been Dad who had left
                         your poor dad
                         how could a mum leave like that?

caught in a circle   hardly wanting to be caught up in that
                         in hating Mum for not obeying
                         in wanting her to be the mum
                         everybody else expected, insisted
                         was what we ought to have   and Dad
                         wasn't he enough
hasn't he always been   tried to be

it's never been   she's particular Mum
was still so full of love

but   yes   had somehow freed herself from being what
she was expected to be, enough to inspire outrage, jealousy
surely

can't hate her for being happier
can't hate her for failing to be everything anyone passing might
insist she be   but it's not that

once again   a line drawn
was that   is it   really   the easiest way?
never realised how much of my life is made up of lines,
commanded to protect
cordons around those who have hurt me
around what I am prepared to live with
barriers around what I am allowed
what is expected of me   what I am capable of

what could I expect   what was I able to demand?
easy to look back now and say
No, I didn't need to accept
No, none of that needed to be trouble

and the lines   weren't they a strange tinted liberation?
weren't they   power, really?
a decision from me   my own dictated restriction
twisted, really   to want severity out of severity

but it wasn't that   it didn't seem like that

It was a revolt.
No longer would I make space, obey, be expected to allow.
I was beyond my brother.   That is what it meant.
                                   That is what it has meant.
But look at him, at how that turned out

firm line drawn between | too late to erase yet

                    desperately   wanting to
how to reunite, now

god   the want of it   what does that prove?
can hardly think of it   without thinking:
Well, this is only because of who I am. This is a consequence
of me. It must be, expected to relent, compromise, bend to
anything and have done, so many times, for so long, yes, I
have, I have
line drawn after being raped, line drawn for Mum, line drawn
for brother, line drawn against who I will confess to, speak to
honestly, barriers meant to protect me, aren't they, keep me
solid, away from all of what it once was but how does it leave
me, what does it give me, what does it do apart from
                                        leave me lonely
                                        desperate, really
that division suddenly bloodier   engraved in the skin

look at this phone

stacked with calls and texts that I somehow can't answer

can't approach   not wanting any of it

not wanting anything,   anyone to think of me

When Dad called
and I knew   I knew   I knew

alongside that
alongside all of it
was a line across my forehead, pulling tight like wire
and that wire had a thought

was a thought

the wire was a recognition
cutting into me
telling me that I did this

I did this

somehow
I did this

I wanted it   didn't I?

I wanted him dead

I wanted something simple
can't be punished for a thought
can't be, can't be
always returning to that fear of my brother
having scared me for so long
built into my instincts   dirt under the nails
                                        always
it is now   I hear
brother outside, scrabbling
it's the death of him   the death of him   out there
                                    in here
the stitched together of him   oh no you don't

I'm done with you, you're done I'm done   enough

the latch juts, front door leaning forward   he's here, he's here
he's fucking here   futilely rotating to a new sight-line
he's dead   he's done   you're done   but the door

My brother.   (I'm here, he says)
And he's through the door.   You're dead

I grasp for words that will upset him, that will make him leave
    You're dead   *You're dead*
I drown him out, I will not listen as he ascends the stairs
I will not hear, if he cannot get through, if I refuse to
acknowledge him, he will leave
    You're dead   *You're dead*
guided by thrill, almost, power in speaking over,

Why have I never done this before?
You're dead.   *You're dead.*

My speech blurs together but the meaning stands out, backing
away, still refusing to see him, to hear him, seeing only a vein
moving to the throb of his Adam's apple, movement, nothing
more,
                                     top of the stairs now
as I evade him   still speaking but
as I try to stop my mouth   not wanting to
tongue moving quicker than I mean it to
I would like to stop but wound up mechanically playing out
                                     CALM DOWN, he shouts.

I can't, I can't, and I remember my brother   I'll crash the car
the ferocity of threat   I will
but he didn't have to   didn't then
what is violence without the follow-through
a fantasy   but later
a lie   was it?
is that it   *Rosa*,   he says
he didn't have to, and he chose not to then, yes, he got what
he wanted, I don't know what he would have done otherwise,
but I was the one who left an unmissable imprint, I burnt
his face, decisive, brutal, it was me

did they look at that in the post-mortem and wonder
what was this story?

marks we carry on

I didn't mean it, I say.
I didn't mean to hurt you.
Not like that, not like that.

He must have looked in the mirror over the years and
registered what I had done to him, unconsciously, maybe, but
something clocking when he looked
even when it was away from his mind,   right there to insist

I was so much more than an absence. Worse, so much worse.

Of course	hands gripped to my shoulders
it can't be	kitchen mirror gifting
	the glint of the back of his head

           John

of course	forehead rooted into his chest
hurts	*What are you on about? What's*
it can't be	*going on? Who did you hurt?*
the permanence	

Would he kill himself?

I will never see him   no longer a choice, forced on me
all of that was real   but now   none of it   he wouldn't
nothing other than this, right here   John, shaking me
                     Whatever's happened, he says,
focus sharpening   *whatever's going on*, he says,
here   I'm here   *I'm here.*

Breathe. Listen. I'm here.

somehow, don't know anything else

what else I have been

what is possible

a line running in and out of focus

clearing   steady

disappearing, isn't it   can't it   John

there is no one else here

not even my brother

Acknowledgements

Thank you to supreme editors Emmie Francis and Libby Marshall; my agent Cathryn Summerhayes and the Curtis Brown team; dream duo Hannah Turner and Phoebe Williams; patient typesetter Kate Ward; as well as Louisa Joyner, Alex Bowler, Silvia Crompton, Sarah Barlow, Sara Talbot, Sophie Harris and those working behind the scenes.

Thank you to Edmund Gordon, Jonnie McAloon, John Roache, Leo Robson and Francesca Wade for, variously, feedback on drafts and background advice while I was writing (plus the odd cryptic email).

Thank you to Mum, Dad, Sam, Matt, George, Jill, Dave, Ed, Dids, Sarah, William and the little ones too: Cassandre, Miles and Evan. Thank you to Alex Lawther, Jack Powys Maurice and the rest of my gorgeous mates, including T-shirt cheerleader Chris Bone.

To James Pulford, I have too many thanks. But as a start: thank you for the encouragement, guidance, love . . . and for how much you make me laugh along the way.